ASSAULT ON THE VENTURE

Dan Shelton

Intrigue Press

For information, please contact Intrigue Press, P.O. Box 456, Angel Fire, NM 87710, 505-377-3474.

ISBN 0-9643161-2-9
LCCN 95-080823

First printing 1996

This book is a work of fiction. Names, characters, places and incidents are either the product of the author's imagination or are used fictitiously or in a historical context. Any resemblance to actual events or locales or persons, living or dead, is entirely coincidental. Although the author and publisher have made every effort to ensure the accuracy and completeness of information contained in this book, we assume no responsibility for errors, inaccuracies, omissions, or any inconsistency herein. Any slights of people, places or organizations are unintentional.

I wish to dedicate this book to my lovely wife, Connie, who is currently working on her fifth murder mystery.

Her unselfish willingness to share her dream as an author became my inspiration. A value cannot be placed on the countless hours she spent in the production and editing of this novel. In all my years of travel and the thousands of people I have known, I have not encountered a finer human being. I am humbled by her. I feel privileged to share my life with her.

The author also wishes to acknowledge the invaluable help of Gretchen Lemons for her editorial assistance and for being the best darn sister a guy could have.

FOREWORD

From 1963 through '66, I served as an Aviation Ordnance-man assigned to G Division, Weapons Department, aboard the nuclear carrier U.S.S. Enterprise CVAN 65.

With the exception of the book's plot, most of the background information is true. Nuclear Task Force One did circle the globe in an effort to exhibit the U.S. Navy's strength in what was called Power For Peace. Whether its intentions were successful or not would depend on whom you ask. As I recall, the Navy seemed to think so at the time. Nevertheless, it was a grand show. I can attest to that.

I wish to say that I have no ill feelings towards any race or religion. Impressions the reader might receive from this book are the same as those they will receive by watching the evening news on television or reading their local newspaper headlines.

It both saddens and shocks me to think that in this modern day of enlightenment people continue to murder each other in the name of race or religion. If I had but one wish, it would be for every person on the earth to awaken one morning having forgotten the words race and religion.

Perhaps then, as the Buddhist philosophy offers, we would all become dedicated to conquering ourselves.

Dan Shelton

1

March 1991 Somewhere near the Kuwait, Iraq border.

The crew of the AH-64 Apache attack helicopter were on their second sortie for the day — if it could be called *day*. Black smoke hung thick in the air. Near the ground, visibility was less than one half mile. Most of the oil wells had been torched by Saddam Hussein's retreating army. It was the closest resemblance to Hell that the men could imagine.

The pilot was thankful for the advanced technology of his Apache gun-ship. Two Turboshaft engines powered it, each rated at 1690 shaft horsepower. Particle separators on the intakes were capable of removing sand, ash and other debris from the air. In their present operating environment, a necessity. Maximum speed was over one hundred and fifty knots if needed.

The Apache's night fighting ability was enhanced by the

Pilot's Night Vision Sensor (PNVS) and the gunner's Target Acquisition Designation Sight (TADS). The Forward Looking Infrared System presented an infrared image of the terrain in front and to the sides of the helicopter. This was displayed on the pilot's monocle sight, which he had positioned in front of one eye, where he also monitored flight instrument data. This Heads Up Display system saved precious seconds and allowed the pilot a constant vigil for the enemy. Visibility through the smoke was terrible. He scanned the PNVS for signs of activity below.

His gunner used the TAD which gave him day or night target sight, plus a laser tracker, target designator and rangefinder. Even inside the helicopter cockpit the crew smelled the burning stench of the acrid petroleum smoke.

Their armored crew seats, key engine components and fuel cells had not thus far been put to the test on this particular helicopter. The two men were thankful.

Their mission: search and destroy.

As he automatically operated the controls, the pilot was caught up in the very same thoughts that have occupied warriors for generations — coup. He had started this mission with sixteen Rockwell Hellfire laser-guided missiles, each capable of penetrating over ten inches of armor. Their effectiveness was now a proven fact. Three had been fired and there were three less Iraqi tanks. Apart from the Hellfire missiles, his machine included a 30mm Hughes Chain Gun mounted on a trainable turret beneath the fuselage, with twelve hundred rounds of ammunition.

During the last week of the desert war, he and his gunner were credited with the destruction of seven tanks and four personnel carriers. If the rest of the gunships were as successful, he figured most of the Iraqi armored division should be destroyed by now. The burnt-out hulks of dozens of vehicles already littered his patrol area.

Almost routinely, they flew zig-zag patterns over their designated area looking for active vehicles. The infrared device could magnify enemy positions miles away, and the Hellfire missile had a range of up to five miles, which helped to keep the Apache away from the tank guns. During some of their recent encounters with tanks, the pilot could actually see the tank crews pouring out of the vehicles and running for cover.

The Iraqis now realized the destructive force they were up against. They hadn't counted on being pounded from the air so thoroughly and with such advanced technology. This surgically clean attack had totally destroyed their plans to trap the assaulting forces into a pincer type situation. The total annihilation they had planned for the infidels had backfired on them, leaving them exposed to the modern technology of the advancing NATO forces. Literally hundreds helicopters and airplanes were systematically searching out and destroying Hussein's entire armored division. Iraqi forces were now beginning to surrender by the thousands.

There were so many piles of wreckage that the Apache's gunner had difficulty locating an active target. He would place his target designator on one, then the next, looking for that tell-tale sign of a hot engine. If the sensor indicated heat the designator would display a brighter green color at that location.

He armed each missile as needed and when target acquisition was received, which was the locking of the guidance and control device on the missile, a squeeze of the trigger sent the missile on its way.

The Hellfires never missed and the destruction was usually total.

If they encountered light armor, the 30mm cannon would easily take care of the job. A short two-second burst could make a Jeep or truck look like Swiss cheese.

To further amplify the effectiveness of the 30mm cannon, each of the bullets contained an explosive charge. Some of the choices that could be loaded included high explosive, high explosive incendiary, and armor-piercing. Each high explosive shell had the same effect as a World War II hand grenade. Definitely an effective anti-personnel device. The choice of ammo carried depended upon the mission. On this particular mission, the call was for two armor-piercing rounds followed by one high explosive incendiary, this sequence repeated over and over when the ammo was attached to the feed belt.

"I think we've got something," the gunner's voice cracked through the intercom.

As the pilot scanned to the front, a contact appeared. It wasn't the strong signal that usually indicated the big turbine powered engine of the modern tanks that made up Saddam Hussein's armored division. It wasn't anything that large.

"Whoa," said the pilot, manipulating the controls abruptly.

The nose of the helicopter came up rapidly as it slid through the air.

The silhouette, now more apparent, appeared to be that of a light vehicle.

"Looks like a small personnel carrier or Jeep perhaps," he said.

They wouldn't waste a Hellfire on that. Reaching forward, the gunner selected - GUNS - on his console as they set a heading to intercept the vehicle. Aligning the cannon sight on the vehicle he waited for the appropriate range.

"Firing!" he announced as he pressed the fire button.

The cannon's scream pierced the crew's helmets instantly as it activated. Every several rounds a tracer flew, making a long line of dashes as the bullets approached the target. The tracers made the shooter feel like a fireman hosing down a fire. The two men stared at the cannon's ferocious devastation.

The entire area around the front of the small vehicle lit up in simultaneous explosions. The smoke-filled air around the vehicle gave off an eerie glow as it reflected the awesome force that had been unleashed. The front of the vehicle below vanished. What remained was catapulted through the air end over end coming to rest in a pile of twisted unrecognizable junk.

"Scratch one personnel carrier," said the gunner.

"Looks like we're getting low on fuel," the pilot said into the intercom.

"Time to get the hell out of here, then!" came the response from the gunner.

As the pilot pushed the cyclic stick to the right and added power, the big machine responded instantly by lying on its side. The two men could feel the downward G-force of the tight turn. Rolling level, he pushed the control forward and they quickly departed the area, heading for their base of operations.

"That makes five personnel carriers," the gunner bragged.

"And ten tanks."

From the ground, Staff Sergeant John Linx U.S.M.C. had witnessed the whole incident. He shook his head in amazement. The Land Rover had come into view about a hundred yards away. It looked as if a mad man was at the wheel. The guy was pushing the vehicle as fast as it would go, he thought. It slid wildly this way and that trying to negotiate the sharp curves and bomb craters in the dirt road.

Linx had become accustomed to the noise of the helicopters as they flew into his observation area but when that cannon fire came so close, he couldn't help but bury his face in the sand. Several Marines had already been killed by *friendly fire* and he wasn't taking any chances.

Judging from the vehicle, that poor fool obviously wasn't military, he thought. He must have been making a break through the Iraqi lines for Kuwait.

He almost made it.

The remaining cab of the Land Rover came to rest not more than thirty feet from John's position. The entire front had been blown away and what little remained would never be identified. Dirt and smoke filled the air all around the vehicle.

As the light desert breeze began to clear the air around the vehicle, the driver emerged, still alive and crawling from the wreckage. The sergeant couldn't believe his eyes.

Raising his weapon to his shoulder he covered the man, unsure whether to shoot him or help him. Fortunately for the battered stranger, John could hear enough cursing to figure out that he was speaking English. Lowering his weapon, he extended a hand to wave the man toward him.

"Say, ole chap," the man said as he coughed and swatted his still burning shirt. "I could use a bit of a hand. Those helo boys sure are hell on wheels. They damn near killed me!"

Sliding into the sergeant's foxhole, he was a sight to see. Setting his rifle down, the sergeant quickly helped to extinguish the remaining smoldering clothing. The man's shirt was burned and torn to pieces and what was left of his pants were smoking. Sand covered his clothing and a thick layer of black soot hid his face. What might have once been a mustache was almost completely burnt away. John helped the man to sit upright.

Letting out a long slow sigh, the Brit leaned back against the side of the foxhole. His white teeth contrasted brightly against his sooty face as he broke out in a big smile.

"Thank you, Sergeant," he said. "It's been a hell of a day. I've just driven completely through the bloody damned Iraqi army without a scratch only to almost get my ass shot off by my own bloody side!"

"What the hell were you doing on that side of the border?" the sergeant asked.

Another big smile appeared and he replied, "Anyone can make a wrong turn, Sergeant. Say, you wouldn't happen to have a cigarette would you?"

Sergeant Linx stared at his sooty companion. What on earth was this all about?

2

Early April 1991, at the office of the Crisis Intervention Group of the National Security Council, Washington D.C.

"Tom, take a look at this decoded message."

It was Frank Pierce, Tom Barnes's partner of ten years.

Big, burly, about six foot two, Frank was in his early fifties and had a thick head of now-gray hair. He was a kidder and loved to joke around. Tom didn't know anyone who wasn't genuinely fond of him, anyone on their side of the law.

Frank's affinity for beer was obvious from his large over-hanging belly. His size had brought him a lot of negative attention from the head shed but he always seemed to come out on the winning end by losing just enough weight to get him through the yearly physical. One thing about Frank though, Tom had never seen him take a drink during working hours, something Tom could easily monitor because of Frank's light complexion. His face, especially his bulbous nose, turned rosy after a couple of beers. That nose was Frank's character in a nutshell.

Tom had chosen Frank as his partner years earlier and had never once regretted it. Being an investigator for the National Security Council was no easy task and demanded total commitment. Frank had come through with flying colors, becoming Tom's closest friend. He had, on at least two occasions, saved Tom's life. Since family ties were frowned upon, neither had ever married. Frank had become Tom's family.

It was a beautiful morning and Tom was sitting at his desk looking out the window toward the Lincoln Memorial. One benefit of being in charge of the Crisis Intervention Group was an office with a view and he felt he had earned it.

Tom Barnes was one of the most successful black men in the National Security Council. He had spent fifteen years in the F.B.I. and had turned a cheek on many occasions because of the Bureau Chief's unofficial viewpoint concerning blacks. That was a long time ago and because of guys like Tom the viewpoint had gradually changed.

Tom could have been a professional football player. He had made a name for himself in college with the help of a football scholarship. Upon graduating from college, he received his degree in accounting and acquired his CPA license. His real interest however, was the Bureau.

Accounting was one of the most desired degrees sought by the F.B.I. in those days and he knew it. Being black, he knew he had to stack every advantage on his side.

It had worked. He found himself on the Bureau struggling his way up through the ranks. It had been rough through the years but he was proud of the fact that he had opened a channel for many other minorities that had followed him.

Later years brought him the opportunity to become a member of the National Security Council's Crisis Intervention

Group. He was now the head of the group and answered only to the Director. He found the work rewarding, enjoying the sensitive nature of his assignments.

He liked to start each day watching Washington stir while he sipped a hot cup of coffee.

Tom rose as Frank approached him. He stood a good two inches above Frank. His physical condition was excellent and he took great pride in knowing it. Not a day passed that Tom didn't work out at least an hour if possible.

The years had slowed him down only a bit, as he frequently proved to the younger men at the gym. The main thing that Tom hated about getting older was his hair loss. He could maintain his body but there wasn't a damn thing he could do about his hair. It was almost nonexistent on top and the light usually reflected off his head to remind him of it. He frequently dabbed that bald spot with a handkerchief.

Dressed in a suit and tie, his usual attire, he felt he still had something to offer the opposite sex, if it just weren't for that damn bald spot.

"What you got, Frank? And good morning to you too," he said.

"Oh yeah, good morning, Tom. It's a message from the British Secret Service and the boss wants us on a plane right away for London."

Tom picked up the message. It read:

TOP SECRET-DECODE XRAY

FROM : BRITISH SECRET SERVICE - Office of Lional Reggie

TO: Director - National Security Council

— In possession of rather important report — Major imminent terrorist threat connected with U.S. Sixth Fleet carrier — Thought you might be interested — Must meet to disclose further —

It was signed Lional Reggie H.M.S.S.

British humor — you *might* be interested. Tom chuckled, although his gut tensed at the phrase *major imminent terrorist threat*. What now?

They left for London within the hour.

It was the typical long flight across the pond. Lional Reggie was Tom's counterpart in London. He was waiting at Heathrow, accompanied by a bull of a man, no doubt a body guard. Tom noticed the bulge under one arm of his jacket.

"Hey, Lenny," Tom greeted his friend.

Lional Reggie was the perfect example of the working British aristocrat. He was impeccably dressed in a dark wool suit with a gray tie. His hair was thinning and gray from the years and he sported a large gray handlebar mustache twisted to perfect points at each end. He carried a gentlemen's walking stick of polished mahogany, capped by a brass serpent's head.

"Welcome, Tom," he responded offering his hand.

"Hi, Frank," he added as he gave Frank's stomach a pat. "I see you still love to tip a pint from time to time."

"Oh cut it out, Lenny," Frank said smiling.

It was a short ride from Heathrow to Lionel's office.

"What's so hush-hush that we had to cross the pond to the land of God and Queen?" Tom asked, as he took a seat in Lenny's expansive wood paneled office.

Lenny pushed the button on his intercom.

"Daisy, fetch the Baghdad folder please," he said.

"Yes sir, right away," came the response from the little box.

Tom and Frank settled into the large leather chairs and began to look through the documents that Daisy handed them. Being used to American habits, she shortly arrived with a tray of hot coffee and tea. Lional Reggie leaned back in his reclining chair and sipped on his hot tea, apparently daydreaming as the two agents began to study the files on the table before them.

The files disclosed that the British Secret Service, after months of elaborate effort and risk, had placed one of their operatives in Baghdad close enough to bug the offices of the

Shiite terrorist planning committee. Among several other strikes planned for the coming year, there was one cell assigned to a really hush-hush operation targeting the people of the United States.

Something so big that the entire world would take notice.

So big, in fact, that the U.S. would be brought to its knees, in the Shiite's poetic way of saying things.

Tom scanned the pages quickly, absorbing details, passing them to Frank.

The target was to be the nuclear aircraft carrier, U.S.S. Venture. The details were sketchy at this point but one more bit of information became quite clear. A deep-cover Shiite agent had somehow been placed aboard the ship several years prior. He was now patiently waiting to be activated. The terrorist's planning committee had been in the process of completing the blueprints for the operation when they were interrupted by Desert Storm.

Baghdad security had become so tight that the British agent had barely escaped without being caught. He was unable to return to the location where he had hidden the tapes to bring them out. His report was now the only record of the infiltration.

The incident would take place while the 'eyes of the world are watching.'

It would be the largest terrorist impact ever felt by the modern world. Tom's insides tightened again. He and Frank exchanged a look before reading on.

Saddam Hussein's forces had invaded Kuwait the day after the information was taped, but the normal channels of communication with London were closed for the British agent. The agent had gone into hiding until NATO forces had taken Kuwait back and had begun to bomb Baghdad. In all the turmoil he had stolen a Land Rover and driven across the desert right under the noses of the Iraqi armored division.

"We can depend upon the accuracy of this report?" Tom asked Lenny.

"By all means," Lenny replied. "He's one of our best chaps."

"This is without a doubt a priority-one situation," Tom said. "We've got to get on this right away. We've got to find this Shiite soldier before it's too late. From what I remember of the carrier Venture, these guys couldn't have picked a more lethal target."

He dabbed at his bald spot and exhaled forcefully.

"Well, Lenny, thanks for this valuable intelligence. I'd also like to personally thank the man that acquired it."

"Oh he's in hospital right now," Lenny said. "A few burns and scrapes but nothing serious. He is a touch muffed, however, at you Yanks, Tom. Seems he had a bit of a close scrape with one of your helicopter gunships on his way across the border to Kuwait. He's top notch, however, and I'm sure he'll forgive in time."

"Well good," Tom replied. "Give him our best wishes."

Tom and Frank left London for Washington the following morning after an all-night strategy session. Neither of them would have slept anyway.

"The director will see you now gentlemen," said the thin nosed, straight mouthed secretary in a mannish pin-striped suit.

Entering the director's office was always somewhat intimidating. After all, careers had been made and broken right here in front of this man.

"Tom, Frank, come in, sit down," John Swager invited, pointing to the two large leather bound chairs that were strategically lower than his own. This, of course, left anyone in those chairs looking up at the director.

"How was your London flight? Fill me in on what you learned."

"Well, sir," Tom began as he handed the file to the director, "it appears that some serious terrorist activity is planned for one of our carriers. We've been told that the agent who acquired the information is one of the best and absolutely reliable. There isn't that much information, as the tapes he made during the surveillance didn't make it out of Baghdad. The agent claims that he overheard advanced plans for a sabotage attempt on a U.S. carrier. He stated that an Iraqi deep cover agent had been strategically placed aboard the carrier several years ago and is awaiting activation. He also added that it was to occur - quote - while the eyes of the world are watching - unquote. That's about it so far," he concluded.

"What carrier is supposed to be the target?" Swager asked.

"The Venture," Frank inserted.

"The Venture? Our first nuclear powered carrier?" he asked.

"Yes sir," Tom replied. "It was experimental when commissioned in 1965. The Navy wasn't sure how many reactors or what size would provide the necessary power to run a ship the size of a small city. Oh, they had all the engineering data but when it came down to it they really weren't sure, so as a matter of overkill, they built it with eight nuclear reactors."

"That's about six too many by today's standards," Frank added.

"Yes, I recall now," the director said. "The Venture. It's probably the greatest collection of destructive forces all assembled in one location anywhere on the globe. Hell, besides the reactors and all the conventional weapons, doesn't it also carry a number of nuclear weapons?"

"It's top secret," Frank responded, "but you can bet on it."

"Well shit!" Swager exploded, "When are those goddamn people going to sit down and actually read the Koran. I just don't understand how their interpretation of the Bible can be so much different than ours! We all believe in God don't we?"

Frank and Tom looked at one another with this sudden outburst. Was Swager suddenly an expert on the world's religions?

"Well," Swager continued, "obviously the potential for some catastrophic event is just too great to ignore so I want you two to follow up on this. You've got a blank check. Set up a team and bring the Navy into this. I'll put the word out through the usual channels to insure complete cooperation. Get to it, gentlemen."

With that the director had dismissed them and was now looking through the file Tom had given him while cursing under his breath.

The next few days became hectic as Tom and Frank used the time to assemble a basic plan. Frank contacted the Navy's internal security department. They, in turn, assigned a Lieutenant Lee Curtis to assist.

Lieutenant Curtis was a young lawyer the Navy had used in several other terrorist incidents in recent years. She was one of the benefits of the operation, Frank thought. Not only bright but pleasant to look at for hours, which was more than he could say for Tom.

Over the next several weeks, the group organized their plan of action. They needed an operative to place aboard the Venture.

Someone with the expertise to spot a deep cover.

Someone with a knowledge of terrorist tactics. It would take time to ferret out the deep cover. Both Tom and Frank went to work looking for just the right person in the hundreds of personnel files of the National Security Council.

Lieutenant Curtis found out the exact location of the

Venture and its schedule for the next few months. It was on a six month patrol in the Mediterranean. It ported in Cannes, France, between at-sea periods.

Tom asked Lieutenant Curtis to rent an apartment in Cannes for the group to use as their operations base. They gathered as much information on previous Iraqi terrorist activities as they could lay their hands on.

The French authorities were told that an investigation into the conduct of some of the ship's officers was underway. This gave the team the leeway to conduct their investigation without too much intervention from the French authorities. According to reports, the terrorists were known to hole up in France between operations. It was obvious that the French authorities had to be aware of this. The less the French knew about the Crisis Intervention Team the better at this point.

The vibrations from the engines of the S1H airplane ran the length of the wings through the cabin and right to the seat occupied by Lieutenant Curtis. She felt as though her butt had more sleep than she had in the last week. She had commandeered rides on several flights from various locations in the Mediterranean in order to link up with this particular airplane.

This leg of the trip was by far the worst.

The airplane had jerked and bounced for over an hour now. She was beginning to wonder if her stomach could take much more of this. Her destination was the U.S.S. Venture. This particular aircraft flew mail and personnel aboard the ship on a regular schedule. It was one of several of its type that flew off the Venture.

"Is this what you have to put up with all the time?" She shouted over the noise to the young crewman sitting in the nearby jump seat.

"What's that, Lieutenant?" he replied loudly.

"You know," she shouted. "How can your body stand this constant noise and vibration?"

"Oh you get used to all of it after a while. Well, almost all of it," he said smiling. "There's only one thing I don't think any of us will ever get used to."

"Well don't keep me in suspense," she shouted. "What?"

"Landing on that thing," he said as he pointed through the window.

A tiny postage stamp of a thing floated in the middle of thousands of miles of open water. It was an unusually rough day at sea and the ocean was covered with whitecaps as far as she could see. As the aircraft descended, the large ship took shape, slowly rolling from side to side. It reminded her of the fat man at the circus only this wasn't so funny. She glanced again at the crewman.

"Oh my God," she muttered under her breath.

"Did you say something ma'am?" he asked her.

"Nothing that would really matter at this point," she replied.

"Better strap in tight now, Lieutenant. Catching that arresting gear is like running into a rubber wall at a hundred miles an hour."

No sweat, she thought, I do this every day.

The minute square on the water grew larger as they screamed toward it — larger, but not large enough. Lee watched the pilot as he maneuvered to line up with the swaying flight deck.

The plane tilted from one side to the other, never quite in sync with the deck. They crossed the near edge, still too high. Her eyes slammed shut as the arresting gear caught, jerking them to a stop.

"You can breathe again now."

"Thanks," she panted.

Her knees shook a little as she deplaned. A Marine met her at the door of the aircraft. She hoped he didn't notice.

The wind was so strong as they walked across the flight deck they had to lean forward at a tremendous angle to avoid being blown off their feet. The fresh sea air, however, was more than welcome and helped to settle her stomach. The Marine escorted her into the superstructure commonly called the Island.

They traveled through several passageways and shortly arrived at a door with a plaque titled CAPTAIN HALLIDAY. She was ushered into a lavish cabin with leather chairs, a couch, and a gigantic desk. The paneled walls were hung with pictures of various high ranking officers, ships, and of course, above the desk, a picture of the President of the United States.

"Please take a seat, Lieutenant. The captain will be with you shortly," the Marine said.

All the comforts of home, she thought, looking around as she waited. It was like any modern office as far as decor was concerned, with the exception of a few large ventilation pipes here and there.

She started to rise as the captain entered the room but he waved his arm for her to remain seated. Captain James E. Halliday was the reigning god of the super carrier Venture. What he said was law and he changed the law any time he felt it necessary. He was considered quite gruff by most that met him and he gave no quarter to those that broke the rules.

Lieutenant Curtis watched him take his seat behind the large desk. Halliday resembled a big bulldog, she decided. His double chin sagged from too many hours of entertaining and not enough of exercise. He appeared to be at least a yard across at the shoulders. His large frame got him his nickname of Tiny which had appeared on the side of his helmet during his younger years as a jet jockey.

Experience backed up his aggressiveness. He had

achieved Ace status by shooting down seven Migs during the Vietnam conflict. Even sporting the extra weight, he still looked quite solid.

He wore his gray hair cut about two inches long. It stood straight up off his head, making him look like an irritated porcupine. Lee Curtis realized she better carefully phrase whatever she said to him.

"I've received notice from the Navy Department that I should pay special attention to what you have to say, Lieutenant, so tell me what's so all fired important that you had to be flown all the way out in the middle of the Mediterranean," he growled.

"Captain," she began, "we believe that you have a saboteur on your ship. He has probably been here several years and could be almost any one of your crew. If we had notified you any other way he might have discovered that we are now aware of him. We couldn't risk it."

She filled Captain Halliday in on the rest of the situation as they knew it. Her meeting went well and she found the captain of the Venture polite yet very stern. Within a matter of minutes after hearing the news, he ordered the head of records aboard the ship to report to him immediately. He ordered him to conduct a thorough investigation of the crew's records, searching for anything suspicious that might indicate the foreign agent. Not to create undue suspicion, the yeomen in the records section were told it was a fleet-wide security check.

Lieutenant Curtis got the royal treatment for the remainder of her stay. She was the prime object of attention that day in officer's country — that area occupied by the commissioned officers and off limits to enlisted personnel. It was rare to have a woman aboard a combat vessel. She felt like a ham sandwich at a picnic. The captain was amused at the control she exhibited over his officers during the evening meal and pondered the problems that a future captain would experience as more women become an active part of the Navy's flight wing. That day was soon coming, he thought.

The airplane departed the Venture the following morning, returning Lieutenant Curtis to Cannes. That was one trip the lieutenant hoped not to repeat, although being the only woman aboard a ship of over five thousand men did have its appealing side.

Meanwhile, a thorough search for the right person to place aboard the Venture to look for the terrorist kept Tom and Frank busy. They finally reached agreement on one man. Mike Young, a longtime agent for the National Security Council. Young had also served a hitch aboard a carrier, making him an ideal choice.

After a briefing about the situation, he reported to the Navy for a short familiarization course concerning his duties aboard. He was assigned to a two man crew which, due to the nature of their job, had access to sensitive areas of the ship. Everything had to look normal. Only Captain Halliday would know about Mike Young's real mission.

Tom Barnes paced his office, staring out the large windows without seeing the view.

"Think, team," he begged. "Are there any other possible scenarios?"

Frank Pierce watched Tom tread the carpet one more time. When Tom turned to face the group again, Frank jabbed his pointer at the easel board covered with multi-colored scribbling.

"It doesn't look promising, does it? We've outlined a dozen situations and counter moves, but we really can't say what those terrorists might try."

Mike Young piped up: "We won't know what they'll try until we know who they are."

"And we won't know who they are until we get Mike aboard the ship," Lee Curtis added.

Tom Barnes stared steadily at Mike. "Looks like it's up to you, then."

Mike swallowed hard.

Four weeks after Frank had handed the message from London to Tom, Mike Young was in position aboard the Venture. Now all they could do was wait.

3

At sea aboard the Venture.

There are over 840 million Muslims in the world today. When generation after generation are born into a religion and never exposed to any other, an entire population can assume a fixed frame of mind. A few might question the ways of a nation if those ways appear abnormal to natural human conduct. Some religions, however, have zero tolerance to any deviation in the interpretation of their writings. Simply put, they have very persuasive ways of maintaining allegiance.

Followers that exhibit any difficulty in believing, or question the interpretation of the Koran, become the subject of immediate retribution. After all, it is believed that the words from Muhammad's lips, came straight from the lips of God himself. It is the Muslim's belief that Muhammad was the last in a long line of holy prophets, preceded by Adam, Abraham, Moses, and Jesus.

In addition to being devoted to the Koran, followers of Islam are devoted to the worship of Allah through the Five Pillars:

1. The statement, "There is no god but God, and Muhammad is his prophet."

2. Prayer, conducted five times a day while facing Mecca

3. The giving of alms

4. The keeping of the fast of Ramadan during the ninth month of the Muslim year

5. The making of a pilgrimage at least once to Mecca, if possible.

The consumption of pork and alcohol as well as usury, slander, and fraud, are prohibited.

The two main divisions of Islam are the Sunnite and the Shiite; the Shiite sects include the Assassins, among countless others. The Assassins were members of a secret order of Muslim fanatics who terrorized and killed Christian Crusaders and, in fact, still take great pride in killing Christians today.

With this strict way of upbringing and total social participation, one can see in the purest sense, the definition of the word — fanatic.

If a Christian questions the stories in the Bible he might be labeled heretic or atheist, but life continues very much the same for the Christian. Life for the Muslim however, can become unbearable. Beatings, torture, and killings are common. Generally the heretic's family will receive the same treatment.

With a system where everyone is under threat of violence, a lot of cooperation can be obtained. With a daily regimen of this treatment, one can easily see the controlled result — a brainwashed order of Muslim fanatics ready to murder anyone, any age, anywhere, anytime, who isn't dedicated to Islam. Living a life of fear, men lose all objectivity toward humanity.

Akbar Abdul Jakmar, alias Ramon Isaban, had also learned to cooperate. Ramon, as he was accustomed to being called, was very dark skinned with black eyes. Of average height and build, he had thick dark hair and was frequently mistaken for Spanish. His dark good looks were marred only by an obvious scar on his left cheek that ran underneath his left eye, a brutal punishing blow dealt by his mother when he once began to act a little too westernized. Several other scars crossed his back, dealt him by his mother with a belt at various times during his upbringing. She demanded absolute obedience.

As Ramon grew up, he had eventually learned to come around to her way of thinking. He had become very proud of his heritage and totally dedicated to his religion.

Yes, Ramon had become quite proud that he was born a Shiite Muslim.

It was a dark cool night, and Ramon found himself staring out the opening of a deck edge aircraft elevator. He loved to come up from the bowels of the ship to take in the fresh ocean air. The carrier was underway, somewhere in the Mediterranean.

The steady vibration, fed back through the entire structure from those ever turning screws, became a second nature feeling. All who experienced this way of life became accustomed to it.

The mammoth creation of steel and destruction, designed to be so very agile and fast for its size, cut its way through the water with the ease of its smaller counterpart, the modern day cigarette boat. Top speed of the Venture was restricted information. Ramon had, however, overheard one of the helicopter pilots say that during one of the ship's high speed test runs, he flew at over fifty knots just to keep up.

That's an incredible speed for an object that displaces over 87,000 tons of water, Ramon thought.

After adding over one million gallons of JP-5 jet fuel, and 800,000 gallons of black oil, used to refuel the escort ships, and over one hundred modern aircraft with all the associated equipment and personnel, it took on an impressive stature.

"Just think of the havoc *we* could create here in the Mediterranean with this ship," he mumbled under his breath.

For Ramon, the most important cargo there was the ordnance. Around four hundred tons of conventional bombs, rockets, and accompanying equipment and, most impressively, enough nuclear weapons to devastate the globe.

Just to say this ship is impressive would be the understatement of the century, he said to himself as he looked around. He had to remember everything he saw. He wanted to make an indelible impression on his mind. It would be crucial when the time came for him to act.

The hangar bay area, also known as the main deck, was about two hundred and eighty feet wide, sixty feet high and over nine *hundred* feet long. Looking toward the center of the hangar, he could see the giant overlapping steel firedoors capable of separating the two massive areas in the event of fire or during battle stations. The main deck stood some forty-eight feet above the water line. The escort ships that came alongside to refuel while underway were dwarfed by the size of the vessel.

Parked next to Ramon, near the number four aircraft elevator, were the ship's boats. The Venture sat so deep in the water that utility boats were required to transport the crew and supplies to and from the beach while anchored in the various destinations they visited. In fact there were only about a half-dozen piers in the world deep enough for the Venture to tie up to.

Ramon tilted his head back, looking up at the top boat. The

smell of jet fuel caught his attention as a vehicle towed a wing tip fuel tank past him. Returning his gaze to the stack of boats, he noticed the captain's gig. The fanciest of all the boats. It very much reminded him of the launch he had once been privileged to ride in. The personal launch of his most supreme leader.

The boats were stacked on large cradles, three high, to fully utilize hangar-deck space. Each of these boats were around fifty feet long and capable of carrying over one hundred men. There were ten of them in all.

The ship was under way for anchorage in Cannes after many days on station, a term used for a patrol area at sea. Ramon could see the bioluminescence, as it sparkled from the disturbed wake of the ship, leaving a long glowing trail behind. The sound of the water, along with the vibration, had a mesmerizing effect on the few men who found themselves standing at the aircraft elevator looking out, each with his thoughts of home, wife, and family.

Or in the case of Ramon, how to destroy all of that.

He was brought back to the present by the reverberating sound of a wrench dropped somewhere across the hangar bay. His purpose once again dominated his thoughts.

He had supported his government's terrorist ideas for many years. After all the killing, though, he sometimes secretly wondered if this was really the way that Allah had meant for things to be. Muhammad had said man must live in peace, that killing was bad, to steal was wrong, and that one must have compassion for all.

His mother taught Ramon that the westerner was unclean and did not represent the ways of Allah, and therefore must be purged from the earth. He was told that everlasting life awaited all who died on this holy pilgrimage.

Sometimes he had difficulty understanding this philosophy. For many years he had lived secretly with the infidels and he couldn't really see a whole lot of difference between them and his people. Of course, they were soft and very spoiled and seemed to always be materialistically driven. As soon as they acquired something, they wanted the next best thing. Life for them was composed of acquiring things.

On the other hand, he had seen the very same response on the part of his leaders in high positions. Better clothes for their families than the average. Better homes, better food, better medical attention. He would sometimes fall asleep at night with his head full of all of these nonconforming ideas.

Usually when someone gave his all for Allah, it was the simple soldier and not one of the high leaders. They always seemed to prevail, to herd the lost sheep.

"Thank Allah they can't hear my thoughts at this very moment!" he whispered under his breath.

He remembered during the recent desert war with the infidels how soldiers were ordered to fight to the death. Anyone retreating would most assuredly bring death, not only to himself but to all of his family. Many thousands were buried alive in the trenches rather than risk harm to their families by falling back.

It was all so confusing. Imagine, his whole life spent to acquire a position amongst his enemy to deal a blow for Allah.

He remembered growing up in Pennsylvania. What a perfect cover. His mother was a deep cover agent, sent to Spain from Iraq when she was nineteen. She was completely dedicated to Allah and committed to uphold the traditions of her sect, the Shiite Assassins. Her dedication had not faltered one bit in all those years. As Ramon grew up she had made sure he knew his one purpose for living.

Early in her life, she was highly trained in the language, traditions and social ways of Spain. She fit in perfectly, easily passing for Spanish. At a time when she thought her chances were best, she had applied and was issued a Spanish passport, and had immigrated to the United States just before he was born.

She had remained an active agent all those years and, in fact, all of his orders still came directly from her. She had taught him to despise these disgusting Americans and to loathe their filthy way of life. She had shown him that through dedication to Islam he could be a part of this most glorious effort to cleanse the world of these degenerates.

She had programed him well, Akbar had in essence, become an extension of his mother, a very dangerous extension. He was without a doubt ready and willing to die for Islam, the glorious cause. He just had to reassure himself from time to time.

He had been trained in all the terrorist methods used by the Shiite, who were famous for their many successful assaults on the stupid unsuspecting infidels. The fools never seemed ready to defend themselves. You could shoot them in broad daylight and get away with it.

As Ramon Isaban, American boy of Spanish heritage, he had "taken vacations" to Spain only to be met by agents from his home land and escorted to terrorist training camps. While the lazy American kids would go off to summer camp each year, he would visit his relatives for *summer camp* and by the time he was eighteen, was expert with just about every weapon used in the modern world.

When Ramon turned nineteen, his mother said he should serve his adopted country and he enlisted in the U.S. Navy. His people were placing him, he knew, for his future purpose. He was now part of the grand scheme.

He was told to be a good sailor and progress at a normal pace, not bringing undue attention. Akbar had actually enjoyed it, although sometimes he found himself temporarily forgetting his real purpose there. He could only look forward to that day he would be called upon to serve Allah for the last time.

It was easy to stay out of trouble. Most sailors loved to drink, a practice strictly forbidden by the Koran. The only problem he had was in not paying proper homage to Allah through the five required prayer periods during the day. With the ship turning different ways, he was never sure which direction Mecca really was. He did however turn his face as a matter of ritual to what he thought was the proper direction. In his mind he would imagine himself bowing in homage. This had earned him the label "the daydreamer" by his co-workers, but that didn't bother him at all. It was a perfect cover.

I would love to see the looks on their faces when they find out, Ramon thought. Someday, I will show them who I really am, although I'm not too sure they will have time to do anything about it.

Because of his mother's immigration to the U.S., he had been unable to acquire a Top Secret clearance, but he had acquired a Secret. That gave him access to most of the ship's sensitive spaces to accomplish his duties.

The Navy had made it easy to get into the right rate, or field. A list was published while he was in boot camp that stated:

All personnel interested in the following career schools, should apply on form DD4687 -2.

Machinist Mate
Electricians Mate
Boatswain Mate
Dental Tech
Yeoman
Aviation Ordnanceman

There it was, Aviation Ordnanceman. They couldn't have made it more simple. A rating allowing him access to all the small arms, nuclear weapons, guided missiles, detonators, bombs, incendiary devices, 20 millimeter cannons and most everything else destructive on a ship, as well as their respective sensitive stowage areas.

He applied immediately and within two weeks received orders to report to Jacksonville, Florida for Aviation Ordnance A-School.

It almost seemed like kindergarten school for him. He already knew more about weapons than the whole staff combined but he kept a low profile, pretending ignorance and carefully learning every detail of nearly every weapon the Navy had on an aircraft carrier.

Imagine my enemy sending me through their schools, he thought, giving me books on every little detail of the latest in technology. America is so naive!

After completing the Ordnance A-School, he received orders for Nuclear Weapons loading school, then Aircraft Munitions School. Completing all the schools with flying colors, he was assigned to one of the Navy's most modern aircraft carriers, the nuclear powered U.S.S. Venture CVAN 56.

What the Americans called having your cake and eating it too. What a Shiite terrorist might call a mad camel in a tent camp.

He had now lingered for two and a half years aboard this ship. When would they release the camel?

4

June, aboard the Venture, anchored in the bay of Cannes, France.

"Hey Matt, where are you going on liberty this time?"

"Beats the hell out of me, Mike, but somewhere they haven't heard of the Navy."

Matt had his foot up on a chair as he expertly spit polished one of his black dress shoes. It was a time consuming chore but a necessity to get off the ship. The standard on the Venture was spit and polish. As he made little circles to achieve the high gloss finish, he pondered a very serious problem he was confronted with. One of those things he had to do, like it or not.

Matt Blackthorn was one of those lucky guys. He was, without any effort on his part, a naturally good looking man. He was slim in build and still looked quite young for a man in his forties. His features were striking, with sandy blond hair and deep blue eyes. He resembled the surfers of the sixties, and when spotted by the ladies, was often referred to as a hunk. The lack of female companionship had never been one of Matt's complaints, until he joined the Navy.

The Venture had pulled into port the night before and a lot of the crew were getting ready for liberty, about thirty three percent of the crew. At the present, the ship was using its three section duty routine. One third had liberty, one third were off work but remained aboard, and the remaining one third were involved with the duties of operating the ship. This way, if the need were to arise, sufficient crew remained to get underway and keep the massive ship in fighting readiness.

"Well look who's here," Matt announced as another sailor entered the shop. "How you doin' Whiner?"

"What brings you to our humble abode?" Mike joined in.

Whiner, who's real name was Paul Riner, was very aptly named. He was probably one of the shortest and fattest sailors in the Navy. The other men joked about how he managed to tie his shoes. It had probably been years since he had seen his feet. How he remained in the Navy being so overweight was one of the unsolved mysteries of the ship. His round face was split by the largest handlebar mustache on the ship. His hat was about two sizes too small for his large head. If there was a cartoon character on the ship Riner was it.

He was one of those sailors that never had anything good to say. If it was a rainy day, the whiner would complain that the sun never shone. If it was a sunny day, the whiner would comment how badly they needed rain. When Riner would enter a coffee mess most everyone would disappear within minutes or suffer a state of depression for the remainder of the day.

He was a first class petty officer. That gave him enough privilege to float around the ship doing mostly nothing official. The main reason most of the men tolerated Paul Riner was because unofficially he was a first rate comshaw man. A comshaw man was the guy everyone went to in order to acquire something overnight that might require weeks, if not months, to get through the usual slow Navy supply system.

Nothing was beyond his shopping list. He was considered the best on the ship. He would stop by to see what extra gear each crew had and to work out trades among the different crews in his division. The main drawback was that if you called the whiner for something you needed right away you had to be prepared to get an earful.

"Hey Matt, looks like you're about to go get laid if my uncanny abilities don't deceive me," he said.

"You'd better believe it, Whiner. One week of heaven away from this sardine can." The second Matt said it he realized he had opened the flood gate. Riner's favorite subject for complaint was the crowded living conditions aboard the ship.

Being aboard the ship for a short time Mike hadn't had the opportunity to experience the whiner yet. He didn't understand the apologetic look given him by Matt.

"You took the words right out of my mouth, Matt," Riner began. "Mike, you weren't aboard then but if you think it's crowded here now you should have been aboard when we were in Vietnam. Did you know in Vietnam, we had over sixty-five hundred men crammed aboard this tub? It was like being at a mall when everything was on sale for ten cents on the dollar. You'd think the Navy would know that crowding that many people into a small space is pushing the stress limits to the max. Someone went off the deep end about once a week. Remember, Matt, when that officer went fruitcakes and was running around the hangar deck in his Skivvies?

"I tell ya, when it was meal time, those thousands of men would stand in line for hours. The lines would start from the mess deck aft and extend about one-third the length of the ship. Then they would wind up the ladders onto the main deck and continue another one-third the length of the hangar deck. It looked just like a goddamn giant worm crawlin' his way through the ship. Hell, we stood in line for an hour for every damn meal."

Mike began to realize this was going to take some time so he pulled up a chair and propped his feet on the desk. Matt continued polishing his shoes as he mumbled something about *me and my big mouth.*

"Then of course," Riner continued, never missing a beat, "almost every other damn thing that we do means standing in a line. The more I think about it the more it pisses me off. Payday means standing in line. Going to the ships-store means you gotta stand in line. Damn, I hate lines.

"Then there's all that privacy we get. I don't know about your compartment but there's a hundred and fifty men living in my compartment alone. You'd think they could give us more than fifteen showers, fifteen sinks and ten urinals. I tell ya, that's one place you don't want to drop the soap," he said smiling.

"And another thing, did you know that I have learned how to identify over ten different types of snoring? Then there's the god-awful smell in that compartment. I tell ya the guy on the rack below mine hasn't washed his feet since he came aboard. It makes me gag every time he takes off his flight deckers."

Matt tried to concentrate on other things. He had endured this lecture on other occasions. He noticed Mike looking at the door to the shop as if planning a quick escape.

"Another thing, when you meet another fella from a different branch of service in a bar or somewhere they always gotta say how we sailors got it made cause the chow is so good. They don't realize that applies to about the first two weeks at sea. After that, our five thousand man crew has consumed every damn bit of fresh food there is. Then comes the powdered this and the powdered that. I guess I shouldn't bitch — they do pump out about fourteen thousand meals a day.

"Let's see now," he summarized, "standing in line three times a day for a meal, being gawked at by those turkeys, the master-at-arms, for an infraction like torn dungarees, needs a shave, needs a haircut, shoes need a shine, hat rolled too much, on and on, then after the long wait, finally arriving at the mess hall to be fed powdered potatoes, powdered milk, powdered eggs, and SOS."

He paused to inhale but continued immediately. Mike tried to conceal a yawn.

"Working all day at the mall, having to stand sideways just to walk down the corridors, banging your head on passageway doors or tripping on aircraft tie downs, going to bed in the evening to be kept awake by sleeptalkers in four different languages and a chorus of several dozen snorers in every key except F-sharp minor, I don't know mates, I just don't know!" Riner took a breath and turned to leave.

"Well, I gotta go fellas just dropped by to see if you needed anything. Don't catch a case off one of them French whores, Matt."

Just as fast as he had appeared he disappeared through the shop door. They could hear his unburdened whistling as he continued up the passageway.

"Wow," Mike said, "with that much wind he could power a sailing ship at sea for days."

"Tell me about it," Matt agreed.

A lot of what Riner said was true. There were times during that first six months aboard, that Matt didn't think he could stand the pressure of living with so many people in such a small area but here he was, four years later.

He was now in charge of monitoring the quality of the water throughout the ship. He had his own small work shop and on a crowded ship that was quite a luxury. After the first year, he began to adjust and felt like he could learn to tolerate the many inconveniences.

He knew full well the importance of what he would eventually contribute. He had made quite an effort to be assigned to this particular ship. Becoming a member of the crew had required countless hours of classwork to prepare him for his responsibilities.

The Venture was the largest ship afloat. It was said that if a person spent eight hours a day entering and exiting each compartment on the ship, it would take about six weeks to visit them all. Matt was beginning to believe that. In his duties he had to enter hundreds of different compartments to determine the quality of the water.

He liked living on a ship that was over eleven hundred feet long and twenty-three stories high. The biggest ship in the world. Look at how many people paid a thousand bucks to spend a week on a cruise. So far he had traveled thousands of miles and visited many countries on the Venture.

It was hard for him to believe that man could build something so large. He had once been down in the Engineering department's M division. They were responsible for the operation, care and maintenance of the four main propulsion engines and shafts which propelled the ship. He was amazed at the size of the drive shafts. Each one, almost four feet in diameter, drove a five-bladed propeller, or screw, which was twenty-one feet in diameter and weighed over sixty-four thousand pounds. The Venture had four of them. They were provided with over two hundred thousand horsepower. Those screws were driven by steam generators powered by nuclear reactors. Eight nuclear reactors.

The Venture was the first atomic powered carrier the Navy had built. Engineers were impressed with the tremendous amount of power, enough to drive the power-turbines, generators, distilling plants, steam catapults, and hundreds of other energy consuming devices aboard.

The water distilling devices could purify enough fresh water from the sea to provide all the ship's needs plus twenty-five gallons per day for every man on the ship. Two hundred and eighty thousand gallons of fresh water per day. And, enough energy remained to power a city the size of Long Beach, California.

The reactors were capable of operating for five years before refueling was required. In fact, Matt knew quite a lot about the needs of the reactors. When they were running, there was a tremendous need for cooling water. That had become his primary duty over the last year. Checking the quality of water to insure the lack of contamination.

He now had his own crew, if you could call one man a crew. Mike Young, second class Boiler Tender, had been his crew now for two months. Mike was a little older than Matt. He had spent the majority of his career working on reactors on other nuclear powered ships. Like Matt, Mike had been to all the necessary schools and was one of the top five percent of his graduating class. All of the ship's company had been hand picked. The average guy aboard had at least a Secret clearance, and of course Matt and Mike along with about another hundred aboard held Top Secret clearances.

There were very few spaces that Matt and Mike didn't have access to, from the nuclear weapons spaces to the atomic reactors.

This had brought its rewards. No more petty duties like being put in charge of work details for on-reps or resupplying. Manning the rail and other traditional duties he had experienced on other ships in the past were out. Matt knew that compared to many of the others in the crew, he was in a good position.

He was suddenly brought back to reality from his day-dream as he realized his partner was standing in front of him.

"I would say liberty is in order from the looks of you," Mike said.

"You can bet your ditty bag on that!" Matt replied, as he headed for the ladder. "I've got one week of leave that I'm taking while we're here and as soon as I hit the beach, it's civvies for me. I'm going to blend in with all the locals and pretend I've never heard of the Navy!"

"That's it," Mike said, pretending to suffer. "Jump ship and leave me with all this shit! Course I can't blame you. Tomor-row, if you check the beach, you'll see a guy that looks a lot like me with his arm around some French honey."

"Oh, and by the way, Mike, I noticed you eagle eyeing the blue prints of the number six reactor void a while ago. What's the problem?" Matt asked.

"I'm not sure," Mike responded. "Something about the discharge valve didn't look right when I did my last round."

"Well, maybe you had better check it out first thing this morning," Matt added. "We wouldn't want to get a little *hot* water going down the wrong pipes!"

With that Matt jammed the shoe polish and rag in a drawer and headed up the ladder. He had one other little unpleasant task to perform. Twenty minutes later he had finished and was on his way to the main deck. He felt the adrenalin surging through him as he walked across the han-gar deck. He could see the line. One more time and then just think, no lines for a week!

When he reached the head of the line, he was given the once over by the Officer of the Deck. He presented the required salute to the officer and the ensign and walked from the fantail of the Venture out into the sun. Squinting his eyes, he was blinded by the bright morning light which he hadn't experienced in days.

He proceeded down the accommodation ladder and waited at the bottom for the ocean swell to bring the launch up to his level so he could step aboard. Grabbing a good hand hold as he moved aboard, he sat down on one of the hard empty seats of the big fifty-man liberty launch as it rolled back and forth waiting to be filled.

Glancing up, he noticed a smirk on the face of the boat operator as if he enjoyed watching everyone struggle as they came aboard. He could see the envy in the operator's eyes. Everyone else was going on liberty while he had to struggle all day to force the launch to do his bidding.

With everyone aboard, the coxswain leaned his head over the side of the gunnel and spit into the sea as if to show his disdain for it. With the wicked grin of a boy pulling a prank he rapidly shoved the throttle forward. The launch immediately leapt forward, throwing everyone into a great pile. As the curse words flew, everyone struggled back to his seat and shot dirty looks at the coxswain. Soon the launch was plowing through the waves with a boat load of smiling faces, each with an air of anticipation, the incident quickly forgotten.

5

Tom sat at his desk in the bedroom of the apartment. The smell of coffee filled the air as he sipped on the local French blend. Stacks of records and other paperwork lay about the desk. He was currently absorbed in the personnel record of one Matt Blackthorn.

That morning there had been an emergency and he had sent Frank and Lieutenant Curtis to intercept a sailor coming off the Venture. Odds against finding him were tremendous but they had no choice. If they couldn't find him today the investigation could be set back a week until he returned from leave.

Several months had now passed since the task force had

been put into effect. Nothing had occurred of any consequence and Tom Barnes was beginning to get a lot of pressure from the Washington office. They were talking about putting the lid on the operation. Hints filtered down that he and Frank were taking advantage of the situation to enjoy a perpetual vacation with all that sun and sand. Two single guys turned loose in the land of the rich and famous.

In reality, however, Tom had driven the group relentlessly. He was convinced that the terrorist threat was true. The British agent in the desert had uncovered the real thing. He had no reason to doubt it. This was the primary mission of the Shiite Assassins. They had to have plans in the making continuously. That was obvious just from reading the paper. Hell, he thought, there wasn't a week that passed that you couldn't read of some terrorist activity somewhere.

His organization had proven without a doubt that the majority, probably ninety-nine percent of the strikes, were orchestrated by the major powers of the Muslim world. The guilty countries could be counted on one hand. In fact the majority of the terrorist's activities were traced to Libya, Iraq, or Iran.

He knew, however, that he wouldn't be allowed to continue much longer unless he came up with something substantial.

Mike Young, their operative aboard the Venture had thus far come up with zero. He had been placed into a particular position that afforded him access to pretty much all the areas that might be considered critical. He was assigned to work on a very small crew which was run by a Matt Blackthorn, the son of a retired admiral.

The thought had occurred to Tom that it would be good to have someone else aboard that Mike could depend on if and when something did come down. A thorough background check revealed that Matt Blackthorn came from a long line of patriots. That he didn't hold a commission was his own choice. Obviously, he preferred being an enlisted man.

Matt's records revealed that he had been somewhat rebellious in his younger years. He had been quite a hippie in the sixties and apparently participated at many of the anti-Vietnam demonstrations and anti-nuclear rallies during those troubled times. He had taken part in the protest committee organized by Jane Fonda that traveled to Hanoi. Fortunately, he had used an alias out of consideration for his family.

Most of the records of his conduct during those years had disappeared while being investigated by the office of a certain Rear Admiral, namely his father. Otherwise he wouldn't have had any future in the military at all.

After much traveling and soul searching, he had chosen to serve his country. Matt had finally come to his senses and become a good citizen. His father had, of course, reminded him of his opportunity for the Naval Academy, but Matt had flatly refused, insisting that he must work his way up through the ranks to best understand the value of it all.

Tom's report also indicated that Admiral Blackthorn had, unbeknownst to Matt, followed Matt's career quite closely and from time to time had taken steps to insure his best interests. His being selected for duty aboard one of the more important ships in the fleet, the Venture, was no coincidence.

Matt had now been in the Navy for sixteen years. His record didn't have a blemish, and Mike Young spoke highly of him saying he felt, from what he had observed, they could count on Matt if needed.

Tom tossed the thick file onto the desk. He had hoped that the yeomen of the Venture's records division, after carefully scrutinizing the personnel records, would come up with something out of the ordinary that might identify the Muslim assassin. The crew of the Venture, however, appeared clean.

The task force group had expected this but, on the off

chance, had to be sure. They had created scenarios for every conceivable situation and a counter plan for each.

The thing that Tom couldn't put his finger on was the statement the terrorist committee had made about their plan occurring "when the eyes of the world are watching." The task force had been unable to come up with any event that tied in with the Venture or its particular location.

They had considered that perhaps the insinuation was related to the fast of Ramadan, which took place during the ninth month of the year. Perhaps the terrorists meant when *their* world was watching. So many options. Without further evidence Tom's hands were tied.

Then it happened. Tom had received a phone call not more than an hour ago from Captain Halliday on the Venture. Mike Young's body was discovered just outside of the number six reactor housing. It appeared he slipped while climbing up a ladder. Coincidence? It wasn't a security area and that left the entire crew suspect. It could have been any one of over five thousand men.

What a mess, like looking for a needle in a hay stack, Tom thought. One thing for sure, Matt Blackthorn had just been recruited — whether he liked it or not.

Tom pushed his coffee aside. It had turned cold and disgusting. Who knows, he thought, Mike could have simply slipped. Maybe he just wasn't paying attention while using the ladder. He hadn't been aboard but a short time and he did have to absorb a lot quickly. He could have had a little grease on his hands and while grabbing a stainless steel railing, just plain slipped.

He could have, Tom thought. Bullshit! He knew better.

6

The place was Cannes, France. Matt always enjoyed liberty here although the sailors weren't always welcomed by the locals. Cannes had been the major anchorage for carriers since right after World War II. Unfortunately, the image of the conquering heroes had long been washed away by such scenes as drunken sailors throwing up in nice restaurants or swimming in the fountains of art on the main streets.

Matt could understand that and had long ago adjusted to the atmosphere. There were lots of other nice places only a few miles up the coast where the welcome mat still could be found. Like Nice or the French alps. Monaco was another possibility. Hell, the world was his for a week.

A shore patrol officer stood near the landing as the liberty launch approached. Slightly intimidated, the coxswain expertly maneuvered the boat against the landing with not so much as a bump.

Matt's first order of business was the traditional ham sandwich, which he always had as he walked down the pier toward town. Looking out over the top of the many white hats as they departed the pier he soon spotted what he was looking for.

The little push cart was always there somewhere on the pier. It was quite noticeable with the blue pinstripe paint on white background and the tiny orange hanging balls all around the sun shade. That little push cart served the best ham sandwich, bar none, in the Mediterranean. He could smell the bread from twenty feet away as he approached the cart. The bread was so hard it was a challenge just to eat it; but for some reason, maybe all the powdered food on the ship, he always started liberty with one.

The old French man who pushed the cart around never changed. He always wore his old sailor's hat cocked to one side, his medals proudly displayed on his chest.

Matt liked to think that each of the many wrinkles on his face represented a different adventure that the old fellow had survived. This was his way to cheat time. Even at his advanced age he was still rubbing elbows with these young sailors. With his robust laughter and friendly nature it was obvious he loved to mingle with them.

Enjoying the sandwich, Matt slowly walked along the waterfront observing all the sail boats tied up at the piers. The first several piers were reserved for the rich. It was hard to believe how rich some people really were, but just looking at the yachts tied up here, he got a good idea. There were hundreds of yachts tied next to each other. It was like the boat city in Hong Kong except this was the boat city for the rich.

He noticed a glamorous elderly lady reclining on the deck of an extravagant yacht. The yacht appeared spotlessly clean. A crewman dressed in white shorts and a blue and white striped shirt bustled about to impress anyone that might be watching. The yacht was trimmed in white and gray with the latest in aluminum masts. The decks were contoured in teak.

The lady was reclining on a blue chaise lounge. She was dressed in a frilly looking pink swim suit befitting someone of her age. He had to smile as he noticed the miniature lounge next to hers occupied by a toy poodle wearing a tiny duplicate of the same pink suit.

His nose was suddenly assaulted by the strong smell of fish as he approached the piers of the fishing fleet. The fishermen worked at mending their nets or doing repairs on their boats. He stopped briefly to watch a man as he expertly ran the fishing line in and out of the net, attaching two large pieces together. It looked complicated to Matt but the man wasn't paying much attention as he laughed and talked to another man nearby.

"Hello," Matt said.

Both men looked up briefly but failed to acknowledge him. They never paid much attention, ignoring sailors on purpose. Guess they just didn't like Cannes being home port for the sixth fleet. *C'est la vie,* as they say somewhere or another, he thought.

Looking ahead, he could see several taxis parked at the cab stand at the end of the pier. The drivers all stood around, each making their pitch at the passing sailors in their effort for a fare.

Good idea, he thought to himself. A twenty minute cab ride should put me in a more friendly neighborhood. He approached the cab stand, about to try some of his French out on a cabby when a voice came from over his shoulder. "Jim, is that you?"

Looking back over his shoulder he saw a young woman of about twenty-five approaching. The closer she came the more he realized this wasn't *just* a young woman but a *beautiful* young woman. He felt his heart pick up its pace.

She was about five foot seven inches, with shoulder length brown hair. She had one of those beautiful faces that just wouldn't allow him to look away. Her figure was slim and shapely and perfectly set off by her tight clinging dress. The skirt was just above her knees showing off beautiful legs. She was tan from hours in the sun. She has to be a movie star, he thought. He could wish couldn't he?

Turning back to see whom she was talking to, he noticed the cabbies continuing their conversation and it began to dawn on him that she thought he was "Jim."

"I beg your pardon," she said as she reached him. "I thought you were an old friend that I once cared very much for. He was a sailor, stationed on one of the big carriers, and seeing the carrier out there and your similarity to him — well, I'm sorry I bothered you."

"Oh, think nothing of it," he quickly said. "I've been looking at a bunch of scroungy sailors for the last sixty days and you can bother me all you want."

She laughed, a musical sound. "My name is Lisa James. I was just on my way home from shopping. I'm an art student at the School de Paris."

"Hi, Lisa," he said. "My name isn't Jim, but will Matt do?" He extended his hand.

She shook his hand as she replied. The touch of her soft warm hand was electric to him.

"A pleasure to meet you, Matt. I have really grown tired of being hit on by aggressive French men. I would really enjoy talking to someone from the States. Would you like a cup of coffee?"

Matt couldn't believe his ears. How many thousands of guys come ashore, scouring every bar and restaurant looking for companionship and finding none?

Sailors generally had a bad reputation and most of the local single girls were afraid to have anything to do with them.

They would be quickly labeled by their own people as prostitutes. There were always those few who screwed things up for the rest.

"I would love a cup of coffee," he responded. "Where would you recommend?"

"My place sound okay?" she suggested.

Matt couldn't believe this was happening. He could hear his heart beating and hoped she couldn't. She said something to the cabby and they were whisked away before he knew what was happening.

In the cab he turned to her and said, "Look, I would be the last person to mess up the opportunity to have coffee with someone as attractive as you, but this is all happening so fast. I get the feeling it was all planned. Please tell me it wasn't."

She didn't seem to mind his question. It was almost as if she expected it. A funny expression came across her beautiful face.

"I didn't purposely plan it, Matt, but when I saw you, I kinda got homesick to talk to someone from the States."

She had sort of a sad look on her face like she really meant it. The smell of her perfume was tantalizing. He wanted desperately to believe her. He sat back in his seat, not quite trusting his good fortune.

The cabby expertly negotiated the narrow streets of Cannes. Lisa looked at him with a soft smile and their conversation consisted of the usual boy-meets-girl questions and answers. For a while he thought they were heading into the more impoverished part of town but soon the neighborhoods began to take on the look of success.

The ride lasted about fifteen minutes and they ended up in one of the ritzier areas of town. The cab pulled into a halfmoon drive leading up to a beautiful apartment building covered in ivy. The grounds were landscaped in shrubs and flowers. As the cab came to a stop under the protected awning she reached across the seat, handing several bills to the driver.

"*Merci beaucoup*," she said.

The cab door suddenly opened before Matt could reach the doorhandle.

"Miss James," said the doorman tipping his hat.

She led Matt through the lobby to the elevator.

They stepped into the elevator, which stopped at the third floor. A short walk down the hall brought them to her place. Unlocking the door, they entered a very fashionable apartment. It was decorated with modern art. Not the real stuff probably, but how would he know? Except for a silver blue carpet, most of the furnishings were white. She must have a thing for white, he thought, looking down at his uniform. Taking his hat, she led him to a breakfast bar near the kitchen.

"Now how about that cup of coffee?" she offered. "Is this your first visit to Cannes?" He watched her move confidently around the kitchen.

"No, we've ported here lots of times in the past. This is our home port during the six month cruise. The Venture will pull in here several more times in the next few months. We have an important job to do here in the Mediterranean. My ship, being nuclear powered and one of the more powerful war ships in the world, provides sort of a peaceful threat to keep some of these middle eastern countries from taking too many liberties, if you know what I mean. Enough about me, how long have you been going to school here in France?"

Hesitating, she appeared to be studying him and, as an expression of acceptance appeared on her face, she said, "I don't really go to school anymore, Matt." She handed him a steaming mug, then suddenly out of context, she said, "Mike Young told us you would be okay!"

7

Matt suddenly realized that he hadn't been invited there just for coffee.

"Hey listen Lisa, or whatever your name really is, what the hell is going on here? What do you know about Mike Young?"

"Mike was our inside man, Matt. He was a member of the Group," she said sadly.

"Member? Was? Listen lady," Matt said, "I want to know what's going on and I want to know right now!"

"That's why you're here, Matt," she said. "My real name is Lieutenant Lee Curtis. I am assigned to the National Security Council's Crisis Intervention Group. Our job is to find those certain persons that might, let's say, have more allegiance to other countries than our own."

"Spies?" he asked.

"That's right. It's still a real threat to security even though the cold war is over. In fact a lot more threat than most people realize."

"Well forgive me for asking, but surely you don't think that I'm one of *those certain people*?"

"Of course not, Matt," she said. "Not Matt Blackthorn, son of retired Admiral Richard Blackthorn, grandson of Chief Justice John Blackthorn. No, not you. The reason you have been brought into the picture is your unique position aboard the U.S.S. Venture."

"Before we go any further, lady, I want to see some identification."

"I'll do better than that," she said. "Look out that window and tell me what you see."

Looking through the kitchen window, Matt could see the half moon drive below heading to the apartment building. He noticed a large black American car parked just across the street from the entrance.

"Are you talking about the black car by the driveway?" he asked. "There are two men sitting inside."

"Come on up, gentlemen," she said to no one.

With that, the door of the car opened and Matt watched as the two large men approached the apartment. One was black with a bald spot that he dabbed at with a handkerchief as they crossed the street. He appeared well built and was light on his feet.

The other looked like a small bear that had just come out of hibernation. He had a thick head of gray hair and a larger than normal nose. Both wore dark sun glasses and were dressed in suits and ties. They both looked very official. He watched as they approached the entrance to the building and disappeared into the lobby.

"I don't like this at all, lady. I'm getting the hell out of here!" he announced heading for the door.

"No, please wait!" she said. "I promise no harm will come to you."

Looking into her beautiful eyes Matt wanted to trust her. He couldn't explain why but he returned to his seat at the breakfast bar and waited. A few minutes later there came a knock at the door and she let the men in.

"So you want to see some ID, Matt?" asked the black man. Both men pulled out their wallets displaying their National Security Council identification cards.

"Special Agent Tom Barnes, National Security Council," Tom said.

"Special Agent Frank Pierce, also National Security Council," Frank added. "We would have been disappointed had you not asked."

They both took seats at the table and motioned for Matt to sit. Lieutenant Curtis grabbed two other cups in the meantime and joined them at the table.

"Before I get started with Matt, Lieutenant, I've got just one question for you," Tom said.

"How the hell did you spot him among all those other sailors?"

"You forget, Tom," she said, bragging slightly, "you're talking to a Navy Lieutenant. Having read his personnel file I knew he was a First Class Petty Officer. He was also a Boiler Tender and I knew what that designation looked like on his arm patch. It was simple enough to pick out the only sailor coming off that boat that had the correct number of stripes and the proper insignia on his sleeve."

"Not to mention that the shore patrol officer pointed him out to us," Frank added with a smile, taking the wind out of the lieutenant's sail.

"Thanks a lot, Frank," Lee chided as she poked Frank in the ribs.

"I'll get to the point, Matt," Barnes began as he turned

toward him. "I'm sure you remember the bombing of Pan Am flight 103 over Lockerbie, Scotland, in December 1988. Over two hundred and seventy people were murdered by a terrorist group. Well, it appears that the planners of that little escapade have something else now in mind. Something to do with the U.S.S. Venture. This time, perhaps, it's on a much larger scale. All we know is that at some time in the past few years a terrorist was planted aboard the Venture.

"He could be working on just about any crew anywhere aboard the ship. We wish we knew more, but our operative in Iraq could only find out that much before all hell broke loose with the invasion of Kuwait. He barely escaped with his life. He was able to make it through enemy lines and across the border to Kuwait.

"I also have more bad news for you, Matt," Tom said. "Unfortunately, not more than ten minutes after you left the ship, your shipmate Mike Young was found dead near reactor number six. It appears he slipped and fell off an access ladder, some thirty feet, to his death."

"How did you guys find out so quickly?" Matt asked, looking shocked.

"Oh, we have our sources," Pierce replied.

"Anyway, we've had to put together an alternative plan rather quickly. With a little cooperation from you, we might be able to continue our investigation," Tom continued.

"Obviously, Mike discovered something or someone who had to shut him up. Unfortunately for Mike, he was involved in many operations in the past and could have been recognized by the terrorist when he came aboard the ship.

"This tells us several things. First, it confirms that the terrorist is aboard or the second alternative."

"What's that?" said Matt.

"That Mike slipped on something," the big man said with a shrug.

"In any case," Tom continued, "we can't take a chance. You're going to have to take over his investigation. We haven't got time to get another man trained and into position. You're about the only other man, next to the captain, that has access to all the critical spaces. So, welcome to the Crisis Intervention Group!"

"We don't expect any kind of move on their part yet," Frank said.

"Why not?" Matt interjected.

"Because this will be something special. Something really big. Look at all their options — anything from an aircraft accident to a nuclear weapons accident to a radiation leak — you name it, Matt. Let's face it, that ship is the most ideal arsenal of tools terrorists could have. With the right person in the right position aboard, conceivably, anything could be pulled off."

Frank stood up and took his coffee cup to the sink.

"They won't try anything until they're in a position to get the best publicity," Tom took over. "Cannes is not that place. Anyway, we want you to continue your leave, and as an added bonus, you'll have a little female companionship. Lieutenant Curtis can be briefing you on other aspects of how we operate. We will also attempt to cram a mountain of information into your head in a very short week, if that is agreeable with you Matt Blackthorn, son of retired Admiral Richard Blackthorn, grandson of Chief Justice Blackthorn."

"You make it sound like I can't let the family down. What can I say?" asked Matt.

"Nothing!" Barnes replied.

8

The second day in port, Section Two had liberty. This was Ramon's duty section. He decided to hit the beach. He had become familiar with Cannes, as the ship had home ported there each tour.

Ramon liked to walk around town looking at the one thing that men want to see after so many days at sea, the opposite sex. It was absolutely forbidden among his people for a woman to even show her face in public. Here in Cannes, there was very little that the women didn't show. While in his heart he knew it was wrong to enjoy looking, his basic animal drive always seemed to overpower his religous obligation.

Cannes is the location of Bikini Beach and most of the European women traditionally go topless there. Many of the men on liberty go directly to the beach and change into their swimming suits. This increases their odds for a successful romantic encounter.

The beach was full of gorgeous girls. Ramon suspected many of them were connected with the annual film festival currently in progress. He sighed as he headed for the bath house. This was prime girl-watching time on Bikini Beach.

Ramon suited up and spent the better part of the afternoon girl-watching. He had enjoyed about as much as he could stand without attacking one of the girls so, changing back into his uniform, he wandered about town looking into shop windows and taking in the sights.

Liberty hours varied for each man, depending on rank. Enlisted men of E-3 and below were required back aboard ship by twenty three hundred. E-4 to E-6 were allowed to midnight and all chiefs and officers could drag in by zero one hundred. Ramon was Aviation Ordnanceman 3rd class or an E-4 so he was good until twenty four hundred.

The liberty boats circled about every twenty or thirty minutes during the day and usually two or three would run during the last three hours as everyone would remain ashore as long as they possibly could. Ramon was no exception, and after walking around all day, found himself having dinner at an out of the way restaurant.

Since everything on the menu was in French, he made a wild guess. The waiter brought him a concoction of chicken and noodles. This place was really quite nice, he thought. He was the only sailor there and no one seemed to pay him any particular attention.

There was a long bar that ran along one wall with tables filling the rest of the place. Hardly anyone was having dinner and most of the people sat at the bar. Above the bar hung a TV set tuned to the news. Suddenly, he recognized someone on the tube. The man was handcuffed and being put into a car. Could it really be him? One of his commando instructors? Observing intently, Ramon watched the story become unveiled.

As someone sitting near the TV turned up the volume, he heard the New York reporter saying:

"This man, Abdul Arup Jonam and two others, thus far not identified, have been implicated in the bombing of the Jewish Rights Center here in New York City. Apparently a car containing a large explosive device was parked in the underground parking area. Considerable damage has been done to the lower several floors and thus far, the bodies of five people have been removed from the debris. A local Muslim leader has also been implicated as the person responsible for ordering the act. Jerry Jaywal, KRBR News."

Five or six people? he thought. What a waste of time. The timing device must have been improperly set. It must have detonated at the wrong time. This was the second occurrence of terrorist activity that he had heard of in the last month and he hoped that if more were to come maybe he would finally be a part of it. This inspired him and he hurried back to catch the liberty launch and return to the ship. He wanted to write his mom to see if he could find out anything.

As the launch pulled alongside the boarding ladder, he jumped across and climbed the fifty steps to the main deck. Saluting the ensign and then turning to the Officer of the Deck, he said, "Permission to come aboard, Sir?"

"Permission granted, sailor," came the reply.

Turning, he headed across the hangar bay toward the port side and there descended a ladder to the second deck. He made his way forward through the mess deck, and then down a ladder below the mess decks to his living compartment.

The men were all milling about, shooting the bull or laying around in their racks reading. Yesterday was payday so there was the usual hot craps game going on below the compartment ladder. Always the same participants, always the same losers.

He turned and headed toward his cubical which was about midway across the compartment. He could smell odors rang-ing from aftershave lotion to sweat. There were the sounds of talking, coughing, and the classy occasional proud reverberation of someone cutting gas followed by raucous laughter.

Ignoring everything, he headed for his rack. He must write his mother right away. He didn't have to. Approaching his rack he could see a letter waiting for him.

"Well, if it isn't the conquering Spaniard," said one of his buddies. "Back so soon? You still had four hours left until you had to be back on this can. I hadn't noticed you loved the Navy so much."

"Yeah, sure," he replied. "I'm a lifer just like you, Smitty, and I can't stand to be away."

The sarcasm was acceptable. The majority of the men hated their present predicament and couldn't wait until their tour of duty was over so they could get the hell out of the Navy. Once you re-enlisted of course, you then became what was generally known as a mentally unbalanced person, or a Lifer.

Smitty sat on the lower of three racks that were stacked above each other. There was a space of about twenty-eight inches between the next stack of three. All total their quarters held one hundred and eighty racks.

On the back wall of each rack was a metal locker where the individual kept his Skivvies, uniforms, ditty bag, and other small personal items. Shoes, polish and other such things were stored in sliding drawers under the bottom rack.

One redeeming feature of serving aboard the Venture, Ramon thought, was the air-conditioning. Most of the older ships in the fleet were not air-conditioned. Here, each rack had its own air-conditioner vent, which was a life saver.

Ramon's rack was the top one above Smitty's side of the cubical. Everyone fought for the top rack. It provided a little more privacy and was the only one that a person could sit up in without banging his head on the rack above.

He climbed up and sat with his legs dangling over the edge.

Turning on his small reading light, he adjusted the pillow and lay back to read the letter from the only person that ever wrote to him, his sweet and innocent mom.

Dear Ramon,

Mary and Nathan your old friends were by recently and said to say hello. Both, including kids, appeared to be doing fine. I never intended to ask them about their ordeal. To understand everything they have gone through would be difficult to say the least. 8 traumatic hours trapped in a car would be enough to make anyone not want to drive again. 2 perhaps, maybe, would be my limit. Enough about that. I know you have been away from home for a long time but every young man must serve his country. He must be patient and eventually that day will come when it will all be over. Everyone has his hour as will you, and I will always be with you even in that hour.

Your Loving Mother

What a nice letter he thought and what good news about Mary and Nathan and the kids.

These heart warming letters from his mom always left him with a good feeling — but not the kind most felt. His was a feeling of anticipation. The anticipation of the hunter just before the kill. Of something about to occur after all the waiting.

Reaching into his locker, he extracted a pen and circled the first letter of the first three words of each sentence up to "enough about that," which was always the end of the message. Across the top of the letter, he scribbled out —man bikinitue8th2pm.

Next he drew slash lines between each three letters and the message read: man bikini tue 8th 2pm.

Man was capitalized and so was Bikini so those were names and the rest was obvious. The message read:

"Meet Man at Bikini beach on Tuesday the 8th at 2 pm."
At last — something was about to happen!

In jubilation, he raised his arms with fists clenched but as he did so, the letter slipped out of his lap and drifted slowly to the floor.

Smitty, on the bottom rack, lay on his side facing outward. He was caught up in a good mystery novel when suddenly something fell on the floor directly in front of him. He not only could see that it was a letter to Ramon, but it was so close he was immediately aware of the circled letters and the message:

"Man/Bikini/tue/8th/2pm."

Totally confused by what he saw, he was about to reach for the letter when Ramon landed on the floor next to it, leaned over, and picked it up.

Their eyes met. He knew that Ramon knew, he had read the message. The look in Ramon's dark eyes was as cold as steel. Smitty almost felt a physical chill. He had just seen something he wasn't supposed to see.

Pretending disinterest, Smitty said, "It's a good thing that wasn't your dirty Skivvies," as he rolled over.

Ramon climbed back up to his rack and sat down. He was angry. He had just made a serious error and he knew it.

Smitty had seen the letter. He wasn't sure if Smitty was the suspicious kind or would just dismiss it as doodling or something. Ramon was worried.

Suppose Smitty mentioned it to someone?

Suppose that someone thought it curious enough to investigate further? Yes, he had really screwed up and he knew it. Now what should he do about it?

Below, Smitty lay still, unable to concentrate on his book, wondering what it meant. Why would Ramon's mother write him a letter with a secret meaning? It wasn't normal. He didn't want to cause Ramon problems, but it troubled him enough that he decided to mention the incident to the crew chief tomorrow and see what he thought about it.

Smitty put Ramon's letter out of his mind and read for hours, something he really enjoyed doing. The opportunity only presented itself while in port. At sea, "lights out" was at twenty-two hundred.

He looked at his watch and was surprised to see it was two o'clock in the morning. He decided that a hot shower would feel great. He enjoyed showering after most everyone had gone to sleep. He could have the whole shower room to himself.

He stood up and, dropping his Skivvies, wrapped a towel around his waist. Grabbing his shaving kit, he headed for the showers.

It was all his, not another soul in the head. He turned on the hot water and as soon as it began to steam, he stepped into the shower stall and slid the plastic curtain closed. It felt fabulous just to stand there and use as much hot water as he wanted, another advantage to being in port.

While at sea, the ship's demand for fresh water was much greater due to its use in the steam catapults and main power turbines. A master-at-arms would stand in the shower area to insure everyone did a Navy shower. Boy what a pain, he thought. You had to shower down, turn off the water, soap up, turn the water back on and quickly rinse off. Five minutes max was allowed. Tonight though, he could just stand there soaking it up.

He thought about Ramon's letter again. What did all of that mean? He stuck his face in the water and didn't see the towel-clad shadow that came over the shower curtain.

Ramon approached the shower, peeping through the narrow space between the wall and the shower curtain. Smitty had his face in the spray.

Taking one last look around to be sure they were alone, Ramon dropped down on his right knee directly in front of the entrance. Reaching his hand into the shower, he swept his arm forward as hard as he could, knocking Smitty's feet out from under him. Smitty's body spun almost a half turn backwards. His head struck the tile floor with a tremendous impact.

Smitty lay dazed on the shower floor. He attempted to focus his eyes but everything was blurred and hazy. He could see someone standing over him. Reaching his hand up, he said, "I think I must have slipped! Give me a hand would you?"

Ramon knelt once again and, grabbing a hand full of Smitty's hair, raised his head off the floor. With the strength of a mad man, he slammed Smitty's head down so hard that his skull burst like a dropped watermelon.

"Sure!" he replied.

Ramon cleaned up around the shower, insuring there was nothing to make this appear more than an unfortunate accident. Meanwhile, Smitty's life slowly washed down the drain along with any ideas he might have had about talking to anyone about things he had seen.

Ramon closed the curtain leaving the water running and stepped into the next shower washing off any traces of blood that might have spattered on him. He returned to his rack, his mind at peace. He slept deeply.

The next thing he knew, Ramon was being shaken awake by two of the others that shared the cubical.

"Hey! Ramon, wake up, wake up!"

"What is it?" he mumbled.

"There's been an accident," said one of them, "Smitty's dead. He fell in the shower and hit his head."

Ramon sat up on his rack and acted as if he was shocked and disbelieving. "He couldn't be, I was just talking to him last night."

"Life is really a bitch ain't it," said the other man. "You just never really know when your time will come, do you?"

"Boy, that's the truth," Ramon said.

9

Senior Chief Paul Zabrinski was in his twenty-second year in the Navy. It had been a rewarding career with some ups and downs but he had to admit that these last few years were the best.

The chief had definite crow's feet at the corners of his eyes, put there by hours of stress and worry. They had first appeared during the Vietnam conflict. He had a ruddy complexion and bushy eyebrows that made him appear gruff to those who didn't know him. His bushy head of bright red hair made him easy to spot in a crowd. With his six-foot-three inch frame he created quite an intimidating figure as the Chief Master-at-Arms. His civilian equal would be the local Chief of Police.

He was generous with a smile and was one of those people whose eyes twinkled when he did so. His cleft chin was his characteristic mark, giving his face a cut of distinction. He was naturally a perfectionist, always dressed militarily right.

He was an airedale, a nickname for a rate associated with aviation. He had come up through the ranks as an Aviation Ordnanceman. These last few years, however, he had worked for X Division as the Chief Master-at-Arms.

The master-at-arms were the policemen of the ship. The X stood for the Executive Department and the X Division was there to assist the Executive Officer in the administration of the ship. Eleven offices made up the division, including Administration, Legal, Personnel, Education and Training, Public Affairs, Captain's Office, Master-at-Arms Force, Library, Printing Plant, Post Office, and Special Services.

It required one hundred forty-one men to handle the tasks assigned to X Division. Chief Zabrinski liked the diversity of it all. Of all his assignments during his career, this one allowed him the best overall view of how the different ship's departments functioned together, especially on a ship this size.

As in any small city with a population of over five thousand, a ship has its percentage of crime, corruption, drugs and other related problems. Over the last several years, Paul Zabrinski had seen most of it.

Most of the problems were connected with conduct. He dealt with all the effects of men living in a very confined world for months at a time, men who had lost their freedom and privacy. Depression, aggressiveness, irritability and inability to cooperate with others were common. These in turn escalated into theft, fighting, homosexuality, absence without leave, drug use, and even murder.

The chief had a force of twenty men. These men were assigned to various locations on the ship and their general duty was to search for infractions of the regulations. These usually consisted of a lack on the part of the sailor to maintain a strict adherence to ship's regulations regarding dress code, hair cuts, proper display of identification, especially in restricted areas, and on and on. There were hundreds of rules that a crewman of the Venture could violate. This ship was known as a spit and polish ship, and discipline here was something approaching a minimum security prison. It was hard on the enlisted personnel but the Navy felt that by keeping the atmosphere very strict, fewer problems could incubate.

That's what the Navy thought.

In fact, there probably wasn't an enlisted man on board that hadn't received an infraction chit at one time or another. After the third chit within a certain period of time, the offender was given a Captains Mast, which approached a summary court martial. The sailor, summoned to appear before the captain, faced sometimes stern decisions regarding his future. He might be restricted to the ship for months, losing all privileges. He could lose rank and be fined some or all of his pay. If he was a repeat offender it usually meant the brig.

Brigs on many ships are usually managed by Navy personnel but in the case of most aircraft carriers, they are run by a detachment of U.S. Marines. Zabrinski hated to send a man to the brig but the man hated it worse.

It's no secret that since the inception of the Marines, there has been no love lost between the two services. Putting it mildly, the Marines hate sailors. A sailor is the lowest form of life to a Marine. The main problem the Marines have is that they are part of the Navy and can't do a thing about it except take it out on the sailors at every opportunity. Putting Marines in charge of the brig is something akin to giving a whip to a slave trader.

In the brig, a sailor can expect bread and water if his offenses are bad enough. He won't be left to sit in the cell all day like a civilian prisoner. On the Venture, he will be forced to work until he drops, every single day.

The chief often delivered prisoners to the brig to begin their punishment. Recalling his first visit there, he had been amazed at the appearance of the place. It was like going into a sterile operating room. Not a speck of dust could be found. The prisoners who weren't assigned to other duties spent their time polishing the bulkheads and decks with steel wool until the place resembled a chrome plated room. Upon incarceration, the prisoner's head was shaved and he was made to wear his dungarees and shirt inside out. Marine guards pushed them about and screamed at them constantly. Sometimes, from inches away.

The prisoners were run double-time everywhere they went. When they were taken to the mess decks the halls reverberated from their precise boot impact. If the call "Make way, prisoners coming through," was heard, everyone using the passageway was forced to quickly jump aside. While running double time, each was required to keep his nose on the back of the head of the man in front of him. They all sat at the same moment and arose at the same time.

The Marines thoroughly enjoyed that job and the chief was damn glad it wasn't part of his division's responsibility. He was content with writing out reports and doing investigative work.

The pressure on the chief master-at-arms was almost nonexistent, until he was told to report to the captain's cabin that morning.

"Chief," said the captain, "sit down and take a load off."

"Yes, sir," Zabrinski snapped.

"Chief, we have a potentially explosive situation." Halliday explained what had occurred up to that point. He related the British agent's adventure in the desert and concluded with the placement of the task force's security agent aboard the ship.

"The National Security Council is in charge of the operation and they know best regarding these situations, but at the same time neither they nor we have been able to confirm any truth to the matter. If there is an agent aboard it's vital to all of us here that he be uncovered."

Getting up from his chair, he paced back and forth as he continued.

"Obviously this information is strictly hush-hush. You as the chief master-at-arms are the only one except myself that is to know. If the terrorist discovers that his mission is jeopardized, he might put his plan into action immediately. As it stands now, we believe that he won't take action until a specific time and place.

"As captain of this ship, I hold the responsibility for the safety of every man aboard. I have elected to bring you into the operation as I feel your normal position allows you to be inquisitive without arousing too much suspicion.

"You have got to find this man, Chief!" Halliday slammed his fist down on his desk. "He can't be allowed to make a mockery of our military system with these insane tactics. I have advised that a policy change is in effect and from now on the chief master-at-arms will be allowed access to all Top Security areas. That includes the nuclear weapons and the reactor control areas.

"You are to tell no one of this and you will report directly to me. Not even the National Security Council people shall know. Remember, you are to conduct your investigation in such a manner so as not to arouse suspicion of anything out of the ordinary. Don't let me down, Chief."

"Yes, sir," the chief replied. "I'll try to find him."

"No, Chief," said the captain, "You *will* find him and you'll bring me his goddamn rag head on a platter! Is that clear?"

"Yes, sir," the chief replied recovering from the blast.

"Remember now, Chief, this man could be anyone, regardless of rank. Find him, Zabrinski! Dismissed!"

The chief snapped to attention to salute but the captain was already occupied doing something else. As he turned to leave the captain's cabin, he heard him say, "One more thing, Chief."

"Yes sir?" replied Zabrinski.

"That sailor that fell off the ladder?"

"Yes sir? Mike Young was his name."

"He was the National Security Council's operative!"

"Oh," said Zabrinski. He left the captain's in-port cabin feeling dazed. The overwhelming weight of the assignment almost brought him to a halt as he headed down the ladder to the main deck. All the way across the hangar bay to his office he kept repeating the question.

"Where the hell do I begin?"

10

Spending a week with a beautiful woman was every man's dream but for Matt it wasn't exactly as he had envisioned it.

Instead, experts in terrorist tactics were flown in from the Washington office of the NSC. His day began each morning at six a.m. with a quick breakfast and then the various experts would work with him throughout the remainder of the day.

He actually saw very little of the beautiful lieutenant, with the exception of an occasional smile. He noticed her looking at him from time to time and he began to realize that she was definitely attracted to him.

The apartment became a training center. Tables filled the various rooms, each covered with blue prints and drawings showing the sensitive areas of the ship. The training experts came and went through the week, each having a turn with Matt. NSC took an additional apartment on the same floor of the building that provided the sleeping and eating accommodations for the men. Lieutenant Curtis took the remaining bedroom of the main apartment. Security was tight to prevent unwanted intrusion.

Matt's trainers taught him what the terrorist's weapons of choice had been historically. In this case plastic explosives would probably be used. Plastic is the most stable and powerful for its size and the easiest to conceal. It can be molded or shaped to fit most any type of everyday container such as a thermos, test kit, or in the Lockerbie incident, a stereo radio. He learned where explosives might be placed aboard the Venture to cause the most damage.

The vast challenge began to overwhelm Matt.

"Just about every technical department has test boxes," he exclaimed in frustration. "Am I supposed to go from one department to another snooping around in all their gear?"

"No," one of the men responded. "Your investigation will be based on the various scenarios that the terrorist might use to achieve his goal. To create an incident the size and nature that these people desire limits them to a specific type of action. In order to do the most damage, the terrorist will have to place a reasonably large charge near one of the sensitive areas. His target will be either the conventional or nuclear weapons or the reactors. You will be looking for any commonly used container, test kit, box, etcetera that has been left abandoned near a nuclear weapons elevator or, let's say, the entrance to the reactor spaces. This is probably not going to be their first choice because they'll need a lot of explosive, but during your sweeps of the ship you need to be aware of such items.

"Another scenario might be a suicide attempt to openly detonate a nuclear device or rupture a containment vessel near one of the eight reactors. He might tape plastic to his body and attempt a frontal assault in an effort to breach the security that protects those sensitive areas. In that case he would have to hide the explosive somewhere near the living compartments. It would be too risky for him to hide it in working spaces, as too many men work in those areas and the probability of detection would be too great. Again, this is unlikely but we can't overlook any possibility.

"You will be visiting the living quarters during the daytime while everyone is at their work stations. We will provide you with a sniffer, a device capable of detecting explosives from several feet away. It has been made to appear like an air quality device. Since your department is water quality assurance, it will be easy for you to explain your additional duties in air quality control." The instructor paused for a breath. "Any questions?" he asked.

Before Matt could open his mouth the man continued.

"The third and most probable scenario the terrorist could attempt is the actual hands-on sabotage of a nuclear weapon or reactor. We must assume that he has a thorough knowledge of the ship's layout, as well as the workings of the weapons and reactors. For all we know, he could already be working in those critical areas. If this is the case it's going to be very difficult to detect him.

"We hope, however, due to the thorough investigations required for a Top Secret clearance that he doesn't have one and will not have direct access to those areas. His only choice would then be attempting access to empty spaces or voids adjoining the sensitive areas. These areas are not frequented on a regular basis, allowing him time to cut his way through bulkheads unnoticed and giving him sufficient time to plant a device."

Matt stared at the spread of diagrams, his head spinning.

"For this scenario," his instructor continued, "we will provide you with the blueprints and compartment numbers of all the adjoining trunks in question."

Lee Curtis interjected a new thought. "You know, there's always the possibility that explosives or tampering might not be the mission. If the agent is really there, and has been for a long time, he might not know his ultimate assignment. He could be given the task of assassinating someone. Perhaps an important visitor."

"That's right," Tom Barnes piped up. "The Venture is quite a showboat with visiting dignitaries often coming aboard for a look-see. After all there isn't anything more impressive afloat."

"We've thought about that, Tom," the expert said. "But we don't consider it viable. Why the Venture? It's got to be tied to the nuclear threat. The terrorist obviously hasn't been awakened yet and nothing out of the ordinary has occurred in several years."

Tom knew knew perfectly well that Matt couldn't absorb all the data they were throwing at him but at least Matt was intelligent enough to become acutely aware. Every night of his seven days leave was spent in brainstorming sessions with the group.

On many occasions during the sessions Matt caught that look from across the room as he captured Lee's glance. He could feel the magic working between the two of them.

The meetings continued to be intense. At first Matt observed the other's viewpoints and their approach to the situation. After several nights, he was participating. They had basically laid out a plan of action upon his return to the ship. He was to make a systematic search of every area considered a weak link in the construction of the Venture.

It was doubtful that he would discover anything at this point but the search would provide him with familiarity of these locations. At a later date, if necessary, he could find his way there with ease.

It was the last evening of the week and the group was gathered around the kitchen table of the main apartment. All of the advisors had returned to Washington. They were looking at the blueprints one last time and discussing the enormity of his task. Due to the location of the sensitive areas Matt's search would concentrate primarily from the second deck down. There were more than three thousand two hundred compartments and spaces on the ship. These were separated by nine decks below the main deck and thirteen above. Although there were thirteen above, the fourth above the main deck was the flight deck and all numbers above that were located in the superstructure, the island.

Frank was amazed at this information and, throwing up his hands, he turned toward Matt.

"It's incredible that you guys can remember where you are and where you're going. Suppose you have to go somewhere you haven't been shown before?"

"Don't think for a minute, Frank, they don't have a good system," replied Tom.

"That's right, it's quite simple," interjected Lee as she spread out an overview blueprint of the Venture.

"You see, each of those thirty-two hundred compartments has a number designation. The first number gives the deck on which it is located. There are two hundred and sixty frames in the Venture. These are numbered from bow to stern and placed four feet apart."

"What's a frame?" asked Frank.

"A frame is an athwartship rib extending up from the keel to which the side plates are secured. The second number of the designator gives the frame number of its forward bulkhead. The third number of the designator shows the compartment's relation to the centerline. The compartment at a given deck and frame, at the centerline is numbered 0. The one outboard to starboard is numbered 1, the next 3. The compartment to port is numbered 2 and the next 4, etc." said Lee.

"Let me see if I've got this right," said Frank. "Let's say a compartment with the number 01-153-3 would be. . ." he paused for a moment, "the second compartment to starboard of the centerline compartment on the 01 level at frame 153."

"Hey! Very good," said Matt. "We'll make a sailor out of you yet. There's one more letter at the end of the designation however, and in this case it will help me a lot during the search."

"Oh yes," said Lee. "I forgot, the function of the compartment."

"You see" said Matt, "each compartment is given a final letter to represent its function:

A is for Stowage

B is for Ship and fire control operating spaces

E is for Machinery

F is for Oil stowage

M is for Ammunition spaces

N is for Nuclear spaces

L is for Living spaces

and so forth. There are 13 different letter designations.

"I think I'll be getting familiar with the Ms, Ns, and other critical areas."

"We'll be notifying the captain that you're replacing Mike," said Tom. "He might not like it much, your not being a pro and all that but I'm sure, due to the circumstances, he'll go along with us. Don't you agree, Lieutenant?"

"I hope so, sir," Lee responded remembering how tough the Venture's captain seemed.

They were all exhausted from the week's effort. Tom and Frank called it quits around midnight and retired to the apartment down the hall leaving Lee and Matt still discussing the ship.

She leaned across the table to point at one of the spaces on the blueprint, intoxicating Matt once again with the smell of her perfume. He raised his head, their faces inches apart. Conversation stopped as their eyes met. They moved at the same moment, their lips touching, warm with the desire that had been building over the past week.

"This isn't a good time for this," she said regaining her composure. She smoothed her hair and stepped back.

"Right." He knew he didn't mean it.

"Good night, Matt."

He watched her walk down the hall to her own room as he reluctantly turned toward his.

11

All leaves and liberty were up the following morning at ten hundred hours. Matt caught the last liberty launch at 09:30 hours and headed back to the ship. He couldn't help but wonder what lay ahead for him.

The launch shot ahead with only five men aboard. The coxswain couldn't help but hot-rod just a little. Matt could tell he loved his job by the big grin on his face.

The roar of the engine was deafening with the throttle wide open. Salt spray shot high into the air with each violent impact of the boat on the next swell.

Everyone grabbed the hand-holds and looked at the coxswain as if to say Cool it, Mate. His return gaze suggested, *Stuff it in your ditty bag*.

As they pulled alongside the boarding ladder, one sailor lost his breakfast all over the inside of the launch. Matt knew, from the look on the coxswain's face, that he would be stuck with the unpleasant task of cleaning it up. The other three sailors grinned as everyone climbed from the launch.

In less than ten minutes the launch had been lifted aboard the ship and set in its cradle.

Up on the forecastle, where the anchor chain was handled and stored, the anchormen of the 1st Division had started the anchor capstan. It began winding the three-hundred-sixty pound links on board. The capstan first pulled the ship over the anchor and then began lifting the anchor straight up out of the water. Several other sailors held death grips on a three inch fire hose, directing it toward the anchor chain, washing off the mud and silt extracted from the bottom of the bay.

"That's twenty bucks you owe me," said one of the anchormen to another.

Sailors tend to bet on everything. In this case, the two were betting on who could guess to the nearest minute when the order would come down to retract the anchor.

Even more popular were the anchor pools. A card would be prepared by the creator of the pool, with multiple boxes called spots. Each spot represented a different time to the minute. Spots were available that covered from one hour before to one hour after the estimated anchoring.

There was always an anchor pool going on. The longer the ship had been at sea the more time to sell spots.

Spots could be purchased for one to five dollars each but in some cases spots were known to go for hundreds each. There probably wasn't a crew on board the ship that didn't have an anchor pool going at one time or another.

The betting, of course, was quite illegal but it was such an old tradition that the officers didn't seem to mind. They usually didn't interfere as long as the price of the spots stayed down.

The tugs chugged alongside and ever so gently began their

push to guide the ship out of the harbor. Once clear of the mouth of the bay they broke away and the Venture engaged its four screws. It slowly began to accelerate as it headed out into the Mediterranean for patrol. Within an hour the ship had left sight of land and life aboard resumed its at-work mode.

All personnel reported at ten hundred to their respective crew stations for muster. Talk of Smitty's death dominated the scene at the Hangar Deck Ordnance crew's coffee mess. Some of the crew who had been away during the in-port period had just learned of his sudden demise. The air was heavy with silence out of respect for their lost comrade. Ramon went about his duties, not joining in.

Each crew operated out of a particular location, their muster station. This was the place where all reported in the mornings and other times that required a ship-wide head count, such as prior to leaving port or in the case of a man overboard drill.

Each station usually had a large coffee pot and wall rack with each man's cup displayed. The cups were considered off limits to anyone whose name or logo wasn't on its side. Some of the cups had initials, some had the logo of the owner's home state. Some painted an animal, like a snake or bird. Ramon's had a camel.

When asked why he had put a camel on his, he replied, "No one else has a camel on theirs, it's different."

After muster, the day went pretty much as normal. Ramon's crew worked in a large void on the port side of the ship at main deck level, fire bomb stowage.

A fire bomb is a large one-hundred gallon container that resembles the fuel tank carried on jets, an anti-personnel device that gained quite a nasty reputation in the Vietnam conflict. Many are more familiar with the term, Napalm bomb.

The hangar deck crew's responsibilites included the stowage, assembly, filling and fusing. A shipment of containers holding fire bombs had been waiting at the docks for the Venture and loaded onto the ship while in port. Ramon's crew had to put these away for future use.

Fire bombs were one of the least expensive weapons dropped by modern jets. The Venture's planes used quite a few in practice qualifications.

Napalm is a type of soap which, when mixed with aviation gasoline, becomes jelly-like. When the bomb is dropped the contents are splattered and ignited simultaneously. Napalm sticks to most everything it comes in contact with. It's very difficult to remove and if burning at the same time, becomes a nightmare. It has definitely earned its infamous reputation as one of the most inhumane inventions of warfare.

The fire bomb stowage void was located on the port side of the ship, about midships. The void was three decks high so each of the containers had to be lifted by chain hoist up to the 03 level. The danger factor of handling the fire bomb didn't take place until the gasoline was added so the work this day was very casual and the conversation continually drifted back to Smitty's death. Ramon made sure to join in on the comments.

In the back of his mind, however, he was thinking of something else. He was angry that he had been unable to make the rendezvous as instructed. He could only wait for the next instruction to arrive. He hoped it would be soon. He had waited long enough and was anxious to become involved in the war with the infidels.

The next day was to be a special day for the Venture. It would be attempting to set a new record. It did, after all, have a responsibility. Wasn't it the biggest, the longest, the most powerful?

This was the day the Venture would take on stores, ammunition and fuel in a long unbroken chain of human activity.

Side by side with the great carrier, the smaller ships took their turns, a line of them bearing food, rockets, bombs and aviation fuel to fill the tanks, refrigerators and storage spaces of the mammoth carrier.

One by one they came and went as they performed their tasks. Using all hands necessary, men from the various departments assembled at their on-rep stations to help lift, push, shove — whatever it took to get the job done.

In a way, Ramon enjoyed these activities because he didn't have to bust his butt like most of the rest of the guys. He was one of the lucky few that drove a fork lift. It did have its moments however.

While approaching the entrance to the deck edge elevator, the ship suddenly rolled to that side and he found himself about to go right out the door and over the side of the ship. At the very last moment the ship started a roll in the opposite direction and he slid right up to the edge. The ordnance chief had seen the whole episode and, approaching the fork lift, began to severely reprimand Ramon for driving too fast.

"Where the hell do you think you're driving, Ramon? This isn't the goddamned Grand Prix! Now you slow down, son. I don't care how big a hurry they're in or how fast they want this stuff moved, you watch your ass, you hear!"

The chief noticed how Ramon's face had turned white and realized he hadn't needed to say anything at all.

"Aye aye, Chief," Ramon replied, swallowing hard as he jammed the forklift in reverse and headed inboard.

When ammunition was brought aboard, the hangar deck ordnance crew manned the bomb elevators, another of their charges. The bombs generally came aboard on aluminum pallets, twelve to a pallet. With his forklift, Ramon moved the pallets to a bomb elevator where they went down to the mess deck. From there, they were again lifted by forklift to another magazine trunk elevator and sent down into the magazines for storage. At their respective destinations, an electric fork-lift moved the pallets off the elevator and stacked them in their assigned areas in the magazine. Other ordnancemen then chained the pallets down. This prevented them from shifting until they were ready to be assembled.

The bombs came aboard without their tail sections and fusing attached. Later, during the assembly stage, the bomb assembly crew would add these.

The on-replenishment continued for hours. That day, the Venture on-reped over three hundred and fifty tons of ammo. This was well above their normal inventory, and several ordnancemen wondered why.

Next alongside came the refueling ships. Ramon was finished with his part and after parking and tying down his forklift, he returned to the hangar bay door to observe the refueling operation. Actually he was supposed to report to one of the crews to assist but he always disappeared into the melee. Ramon was generally known as a *skater*.

Ramon loved to watch the high-line operation. As each ship came alongside, a boatswains mate would begin the operation by shooting a large caliber shotgun with a plastic device sticking out of it at the other ship. Attached to the plastic device was a very strong nylon string. It uncoiled with amazing speed and the device flew cross the main deck of the other ship. The string would be grabbed by the crew of the other ship and they pulled in as the crew on the Venture let out.

At the end of the string a small rope was attached and that, too, was drawn across. This process continued, with a little larger rope attached each time, until a cable from a winch on the carrier was drawn across to the other ship. The cable would then be attached to a winch on the other ship. There was a hoisting eye on the cable and, as the winch operator made slack on the carrier side, the winch operator on the other ship took up the slack.

This appeared to Ramon as quite a challenge. It required coordination on the part of not only the winch operators but the captains of both ships. Each captain had to maintain his respective speed and distance from the other ship. It was far from a perfected procedure and if the swells were very large, many of the loads of material would be suddenly dipped into the ocean. On many occasions valuable cargoes were claimed by King Neptune. On this day, one of the mail bags was lost.

Most personnel arriving on the carrier at sea were flown aboard but in the case of the smaller ships without helidecks, the notorious boatschair was used.

The traveler would be strapped into the boatschair which was suspended on the high-line. He would be high-lined across the open expanse between the ships.

On occasion Ramon had witnessed the sacrificial dipping of the chair into the salty brine. All it took was a roll of one ship in the direction of the other to slack the line or perhaps one winch operator slacking off faster than the other took in, and the chair plunged into the sea.

Ramon had heard of times when the passengers had been torn from the chair while submerged. This operation was obviously limited to very good sea conditions. It was one of the more popular viewing pastimes by those otherwise not occupied.

"One thing's for sure," he said quietly. "If you were an infidel in the chair, you wouldn't want a Shiite operating the winch."

While all of this progressed, more supplies were air lifted by the helicopters as they shuttled supplies from the small helidecks on the support ships to the flight deck of the carrier.

Turning to look inboard, Ramon watched the human ant farm. Thousands of sailors moved about, each in a different direction with a different purpose. Stacks of cardboard boxes, wooden food crates, metal bomb fin containers, rope, cable, nets, handling equipment, and technical equipment were piled everywhere.

Extending from the huge stacks of supplies and running across the hangardeck were long aluminum conveyors. These were long rails with countless metal wheels between. Each ended up at some elevator or actually went down companion ways to the decks below. It appeared like a giant road map with aluminum roads running every way. The sound of the rollers as the boxes flew on their way to their respective destinations, along with the sound of men yelling and the many different types of equipment being used, was all amplified by the cavern-like hangar bay. The effect was deafening and Ramon couldn't wait to hear the command: "Secure from On-rep stations - I repeat - Secure from On-rep."

The last ship finally broke away and the men spent the next several hours stowing the remaining cargo left on the hangar deck.

An hour later Ramon was eating some of the fresh food he had helped bring aboard and wondering where they had found mangoes around the Mediterranean.

That night as he was drifting off to sleep, he couldn't help but worry that an important message from his mom had been in that mail sack.

"What do you suppose they have planned for you, Ramon?" he said under his breath.

12

Chief Zabrinski sat at his desk in the master-at-arms office. He had been there for hours going over paper work. He decided to refer a lot of his duties to the assistant master-at-arms so he could spend more time organizing his search for the terrorist.

A list of all personnel that had come aboard the ship in the last twelve months lay in front of him. There were over six hundred new arrivals. He had gone up and down and back and forth through the list but nothing looked out of the ordinary.

There were transfers from other ships, transfers from Naval air stations, new arrivals from "A" schools, "B" schools — it was endless. Besides, who was to say when this man came aboard the ship? Hell, he could have been here twenty-four months for all they knew. He requested the computers to supply him with any names that sounded like they might be of Arabic origin. He got zero.

He decided to start a systematic tour of the ship as the captain had suggested. He began each morning, after muster, with a visit to areas that he hadn't had access to until now. He would spend about two hours each day doing this. It was very enlightening but again, nothing out of the ordinary.

He had returned to the scene of Mike Young's accident. Since discovering who Mike Young was, the accident now had a whole new meaning. Zabrinski climbed up and down the ladder a dozen times trying to imagine what might have taken place.

The body was in the morgue but scheduled to be flown off soon. In fact, the only reason it was still on board was at his insistence. He wanted an autopsy performed but was informed it would have to be done ashore.

There was a doctor on board who had experience in pathology in the past so Zabrinski asked for a few minutes of the man's time. He was told to call back in a day or so.

Irritated, the chief called the captain for assistance. Within minutes, his phone rang.

"Chief Zabrinski, please."

"Speaking."

"Chief, this is Dr. Thompson at sick bay. I find myself with some free time. What can I do for you?"

H Division hospital was located on the second deck about amidships. It was headed by Commander Joe Thompson, Jr., MC, USN, one of the Navy's foremost Aviator Flight Surgeons. He had a staff of six doctors specializing in aviation medicine, surgery, radio biology, and internal medicine.

They were ably assisted by a medical administrative assistant and fifty hospital corpsmen. The Venture's sick bay had eighty-six beds and was on par with many metropolitan hospitals. It was equipped with the best in laboratory, operating, x-ray, EKG, audiometric, and physiotherapy facilities. The pharmacy filled over twelve thousand prescriptions a year. It was a busy place and the chief could see why the commander didn't want to take time out to discuss an accident victim, if it was an accident.

A half hour later they were at the morgue. The ship was only equipped to handle a few bodies on a temporary basis.

"Doctor, I would like you to examine the body of Mike Young, the the man who fell several days ago."

"Chief, I did have a look at him the other day and I didn't see anything unusual. After apparently slipping off the ladder, he fell about thirty feet landing face down on the deck. His right arm was broken between the wrist and the elbow and he sustained a skull fracture. Obviously, it was the skull fracture that killed him."

He opened the door to the refrigerated compartment and pulled the tray out. The remains of Mike Young were now in a body bag and tagged. As he continued talking, he unzipped the bag the full length and pulled it open.

"What are all the lines running across his face on the right, Doctor?"

"Those are impressions made by the grating where the body lie until discovered. You see, after the heart stops beating the blood settles in the lower extremities of the body. This is called pooling. In this case, the lower right side of the face was an accumulation area and made the lines stand out even more than usual. I'm not entirely sure how the arm was broken. One of the other doctors responded when the call came in. He said he wasn't sure of that either. The arm was folded under the body. It definitely received a hard blow from something."

The chief noticed a mark on Young's forehead.

"What is the strange half moon shape on the top of his forehead?" he asked.

"We think that he probably stood up on the platform above

the ladder and struck his head, causing him to lose his balance. He fell backwards, perhaps striking his arm on the retention railing. Anyway, with our limited facilities that's about the best conclusion we've been able to reach."

Looking once again at the mark on Young's forehead, the chief thanked the commander for his time.

"I've been informed that the body remains until you give the okay, Chief. We really need the space and . . ."

"Oh sure, Commander, by all means feel free. I've seen what I wanted. Thank you again."

With that, Zabrinski left the sick bay. On his way back to his office he kept seeing the half moon mark with the little dots paralleling the inside of the curve. Where had he seen that before? Deciding to try out the doctor's supposition, he returned to the scene of the fall.

Climbing the ladder, he began to look around for an object that might have caused the imprint on Young's forehead. There was nothing. Squatting down he looked lower. Still nothing. If Mike raised up and struck his head on something, it had to be here. Still nothing. Maybe their premise was wrong. He started back down the ladder. Just as his face drew even with the railing it came to him.

The design didn't come from something Mike hit his head on. It came from something that hit his head.

He remembered where he had seen that design. Where everyone sees that design every day. All one has to do is look down as they walk across the hangar deck, to see the heel prints from someone stepping in a little oil or water. It was the impression left by the heel of a dress shoe. Each officer and sailor on the ship is issued a pair. Climbing back up, he began to put the picture together.

Mike Young was climbing the ladder.

He didn't fall, he was kicked off the ladder.

One thing didn't make sense however, from the location of

the mark on his forehead. Zabrinski didn't think the blow was direct enough to knock Mike loose. He wouldn't have been climbing the ladder with one hand.

Or would he? Maybe he wasn't climbing with one hand but suppose he just had one hand on the ladder. It was coming to him now. He could see the event slowly unfolding.

"If I'm right . . . ," he said out loud as he looked around.

Not more than four feet in front of him was a water tight door and hanging next to it an emergency box-end dogging wrench. The wrench was used in the event the handles became jammed and couldn't be moved by hand. Removing his handkerchief, Zabrinski wrapped it around the tip of the handle and pulled the wrench free from the bracket. Looking it over closely, he noticed what appeared to be some skin and blood about an inch from the end of the box end.

The scene unfolded in shocking clarity. Mike Young climbed the ladder. When his head reached about knee high to the deck above him, he must have seen someone standing there. Someone in the act of swinging the wrench downward toward him. Mike's natural reaction would be to raise his arm to ward off the blow — thus the broken arm.

Holding on with the remaining hand, out of balance, and in the ideal position to receive a kick, he was literally booted into space. That explained why his body landed several feet in front of the ladder. Anyone falling off a vertical ladder would end up directly at the base of the ladder, not three feet away.

Chief Zabrinski let out a low whistle. Mike's death was no accident. It was murder.

"If I'm lucky," he said out loud, "there will be a set of prints on this wrench that will identify the murderer."

13

Matt's mustering station was tucked deep within the heart of the Venture. He was actually assigned to the Reactor Laboratory Division. His general areas of concern were the control of radiological hazards to personnel and the control of corrosion within the reactor system. The Reactor Laboratory Division maintained the standards necessary for exacting control in these areas. Matt worked in the department for two years before getting the opportunity to have his own shop.

The RL department was also responsible for maintaining a radiological watch on all water systems on the ship. This small part of the department had little demand for manpower so when his predecessor retired, Matt jumped on the opportunity to take over his position.

Matt's rating was Boiler Tender and normally he would have been assigned to a conventionally powered ship but Matt had, this one time, approached his father for help. He wanted to be part of the *new Navy,* the nuclear powered future. Admiral Blackthorn had only to make one phone call and Matt's future in nuclear reactors was assured.

Matt had undergone extensive training, not only as a regular *nuke*, but also in the specialized fields of water chemistry and radiological controls. In these fields, he was the Navy's expert.

The personnel of RL division were called ELT's, Engineering Laboratory Technicians, and the Division itself was sometimes referred to as the ELT Gang. The gang worked twenty-four hours a day, seven days a week, whether in port or at sea.

The Venture had eight nuclear reactors, and although they represented fantastic technology, their very nature made necessary the modern disciplines that gave purpose to the world's only Reactor Laboratory Division.

The primary concern of Matt's small shop was radiological safety to personnel. Prior to moving to his small shop, his major duty in the ELT gang had been monitoring the chemistry of the water that was used in the reactor plants. Now he monitored the chemistry of the water throughout the ship.

Matt was required to understand all the plumbing going to and coming from the reactors. There had been occurrences in the past when, after repairs of one kind or another, a sailor had turned on the salt water and received fresh water or the contrary. He had even seen a case when sewage came out. Some would have sworn that it was impossible but it had happened.

There were, after all, two hundred and thirty miles of pipe and tubing used in the construction of this ship and there would always be human error. Thus far he had not monitored any radiation in any of the water systems.

His job took him, primarily, to the compartments nearest the reactor spaces. He checked heads and deep-sinks, taking samples, labeling them, and returning them to his small ten-by-ten foot shop for testing. He had created a schedule of tests that he strictly followed, giving himself an assured period between checks.

Since he was now looking for *other things* he became more aware of his surroundings. The diversity of his new duties would have been quite a refreshing break from the normal humdrum, were the situation not overshadowed by the terrorist threat.

He wondered just what the reaction of the crew might be if they suddenly found out that one of their shipmates was a Shiite Assassin just casually kicking back waiting for the opportunity to, perhaps, blow them all to hell.

Matt became acutely aware of Chief Zabrinski's presence. It seemed like everywhere he turned, he ran into the chief, even in restricted areas. He felt almost sure the chief didn't hold that level security clearance.

At muster the next morning he made the comment to one of the ELT gang.

"I've noticed the master-at-arms snooping around the restricted areas lately. I thought this was off limits for him."

"It was," replied his coworker, "but a new policy came down, all the way from the Old Man. It seems the captain has ordered a ship-wide security check just to keep everyone on their toes and the chief is conducting it. I hear they even gave him clearance to the nuclear weapons area."

"Interesting," replied Matt.

If I were the terrorist, Matt thought, wouldn't I try to get myself into a position of total access? Wouldn't it be convenient to be the master-at-arms as well? This could be the guy.

The ship would be returning to Cannes in a few days and he decided to report his suspicions to Tom Barnes. His mind raced. Since the order for the ship-wide security check came directly from the captain, could he also be in on the plot? No,

Matt told himself, that's going too far. On the other hand, the chief couldn't have ordered the check.

"Man," he whispered, "what a bag of worms."

14

The master-at-arms office was located on the 01 level, aft port side. The chief had just walked in the door when the assistant master-at-arms, Jack Johnson, looked up from his pile of paper work.

"Hi, Chief," he said. "What's with the dogging wrench? "

"A lot I hope," the chief replied proudly.

"You've got my attention, Chief."

"That accidental fall the other day wasn't an accident at all," the chief replied.

"What do you mean, Chief? I talked with the doctor at the scene and it was his impression that the guy stood up and banged his head on something, which sent him tumbling over the rail."

"No way," the chief smirked. "See this wrench? Well, somebody was standing above the ladder and just about the time Young got to the top, he was struck and then kicked off the ladder. No, he didn't fall at all. I'd bet a month's pay that when we get this wrench back from the Navy finger-print lab, we'll have a good set of prints along with some tissue and blood samples that match the victim's.

"Johnson, I want you to prepare the paper work for this wrench and get it on the next flight out. Tell the lab we want the results back as soon as possible."

Zabrinski was feeling pretty good. At least they had a lead. He wished he had been one of the first at the scene when Young's fall occurred. He felt that a lot could have been learned by the position of the body. Johnson and the duty M.D. had investigated both of the last two deaths.

The chief had been on liberty on both occasions.

Funny thing, he thought, two deaths within forty-eight hours of each other. They appeared totally unrelated. Strange though, to have two fatal accidents so close together, after going for over a year without anything. Normally he would have dismissed it but under the circumstances, he couldn't.

"Johnson, let me have the accident file on that other sailor . . . what was his name?"

"It was Arnold Smith," Johnson replied. "Arnold J. Smith."

"Brief me on the incident while you're looking," said Zabrinski. He sat down at his desk and carefully laid the wrench down.

"Well Chief, when the duty master-at-arms for that area, . . . let's see," he paused, "ah yes, that was Jones. When Jones made his rounds through the ordnance compartment head, about 03:00 that morning, he heard the shower running. He made a sweep through the head and then a round through the compartment. He reported that everything was quiet except for the usual snoring. As he passed the head door he noticed the same shower still running, so he stepped up to it and tapped on the bulkhead next to the shower. He told whoever it was that they'd been in there long enough and to finish it up and get out. He said he got no reply, so he repeated it louder. Still no reply so he stuck the night-stick through the curtain and pulled it open. That's when he found the guy laying there."

"Afternoon, what's up?" said Jones as he entered the master-at-arms office.

"Speak of the devil," said Johnson.

"Yeah," said the chief, "just the man I want to talk to."

"What can I do for you, Chief? " replied Jones.

"Tell me about discovering the guy, Smith," the chief said.

"Well, Chief, this guy was in the shower in the Ordnance Department head when I found him. I had already made a round through there and when I noticed he was still in the shower, I told him to get out. He was using too much water. When he didn't answer me, I told him again. Still no answer so I pushed the curtain open with my stick and there he was laying on the tile, his head split open and his feet straight up in the air."

"What do you mean, his feet straight up in the air?" the chief queried.

"Well Chief, both his heels were resting on the bulkhead just below the tap handles and his back was flat on the floor."

"Did you notice anything else, Jones?"

"Not a thing, Chief. I called the office and somebody got Johnson up. He came down and wrote the preliminary report."

"Thanks, Jones. If I need something else I'll let you know."

"Sure, Chief. I'm out of here, I'll see you later."

His feet straight up in the air, the chief thought, how strange.

"It's seventeen hundred Johnson, I'm out of here myself. Make sure you do the paper work on the wrench and get it out ASAP."

"You bet, Chief, right away," Johnson replied.

95

With that, the chief headed for the chief's mess for the evening meal.

Johnson completed the paper work on the wrench and was about to place the wrench in a plastic bag when his relief AE3 Roper arrived. Setting the box of plastic bags down on the table he began briefing his relief. He laid the paper work on top of the wrench. As he was talking to Roper, the ventilation blower came on. Neither of the two noticed as the request for the finger-print check was blown off the wrench and, doing about a half loop, became lodged between the bulkhead and a filing cabinet. As Johnson walked out the door he said over his shoulder to Roper, "The chief seemed pretty fired up about that wrench, so take care of it right away."

"Yeah okay," the relief replied automatically.

Turning toward the chief's desk, Roper saw the dogging wrench lying there and assumed the chief was probably pissed about somebody leaving it there. He picked up the wrench and, looking around, noticed the water tight door across the room was missing its wrench. He walked across to the wrench bracket and casually replaced it. Only a very small corner of the request form protruded from behind the back of the file cabinet.

"What's the big deal about a wrench?" Roper muttered. "Wonder why the hell he didn't do it himself?"

After chow the chief returned to his quarters to retire. He was one of those people that easily got ulcers. When something was on his mind, he couldn't let go. All that had transpired since his visit to the captain constantly ran through his mind.

Ah well, he thought. It's been a long day, enough is enough.

Grabbing his shaving gear and towel, he headed for a hot shower. Standing there in the hot shower felt like a million bucks. He always washed his hair first so he shampooed up a good lather. With his eyes closed he set the shampoo bottle down, accidentally, on top of the soap dish. The bar of soap shot out of the tray and landed on the tile floor. With Zabrinski's next step, his feet flew backward, his knees striking the front of the shower stall.

He picked himself up slowly. Clumsy, he thought. I'd better learn to be more careful or I might end up . . . with my legs pointing straight up in the air. . .

He glanced around the shower stall. There was no way a person could slip in that small space and strike his head on the tile floor. He might bust his butt. He might hit his head on the back of the shower but that wouldn't kill him. How the hell did Smith end up the way he did, upside down?

Zabrinski finished his shower and went to bed, facing a sleepless night.

The next day, the chief paid a little visit to the scene of Smith's accident, the ordnance crew's head. He wanted to compare the size of their shower with the one in the chief's quarters. They were the same.

His nagging doubt clenched into a fiery ball in his stomach.

He knew from the report that Smith was a member of the hangar deck ordnance crew. He decided to stop by the hangar deck crew's coffee mess and snoop around. A quick check of the ship's phone book indicated that it was located on the aft port side on the main deck. It wasn't far from his office and took him only a few minutes to get there. As he walked in, he saw several of the guys sitting around drinking coffee and smoking cigarettes. The once-white walls now had a yellow tinge from the countless hours of exposure to the smoking. There was a large coffee pot on a table along the bulkhead and all the crew coffee cups hung just above.

"Good morning, gentlemen," the chief said.

"Morning, Chief," one of them replied. "What can we do you for? " he grinned.

"We're out of coffee at our mess," the chief replied. "Can I bum a cup from you? "

"Sure, Chief, help yourself, the visitor's cup is the plain one on the bottom right side."

Taking the one indicated, he filled it and took a seat on the wooden bench across from the cup rack. He took a slug of the coffee and almost came unglued. Most of the crew smiled, and one said, "We kinda like it strong, Chief. It helps us fire up for the day."

"It should," the chief replied, grinning. He stared at the ferocious brew in his mug. "By the way, what can you guys tell me about the death of your shipmate, Smith?"

"You probably know as much as we do about it, Chief," one replied. "We heard he fell in the shower and smacked his head and that's about all. Right fellows?"

"Yeah, that's what I heard," said another.

The third nodded his head in agreement.

"What about his state of mind? Was he depressed? Did he seem distracted? Did he mention to anyone any problems he was having?"

"What are you getting at, Chief?"

"Oh, I just thought that if he were distracted enough by something, it might have made him a bit more careless."

"Chief, you should talk to *the day dreamer*. He sleeps in the same cubical that Smitty was in."

"The day dreamer?"

"Oh yeah Chief, sorry, that's what we call Ramon 'cause he's always staring out into space. Ramon Isaban, that's who you want to talk to."

"The morning after Smitty's accident, I woke Ramon up and told him. I remember him making a comment that he was talking to Smitty the night before."

"Where can I find Ramon about this time of morning?" the chief asked.

"Did I hear my name mentioned?" Ramon said, stepping through the door of the coffee mess.

"Chief, if you don't need us any more, we've got to get to work. Ramon can catch up with us when you're finished with him," the crew leader stated.

"Thanks for the help guys," Zabrinski replied.

"Ramon," the crew leader said as they were walking out, "the chief master-at-arms wants to ask you about Smitty."

Ramon went cold as he heard the words.

"Sure, Chief, what can I tell you? " he said, forcing his voice to remain normal.

Ramon grabbed his cup off the rack and, pouring himself a cup of coffee, he turned facing the chief. Raising the cup to his lips, he took his first slug of coffee for the day.

Asking Ramon about Smitty, Zabrinski sat back and listened to Ramon's responses. Even more interesting, though, was his appearance. Black hair, heavy eyebrows and olive skin. He made a mental note of the camel design on Ramon's mug. Interesting choice.

Ramon, like all the others claimed to have no knowledge of Smitty's state of mind at the time of the accident. Zabrinski didn't care. He had just used that "state of mind" stuff as an excuse anyway.

Returning to his office, he had Jack go to the records office and get Ramon's file. Grabbing a cup of coffee he sat down to read.

Most of the information in Ramon's file was the usual stuff found in all personnel jackets. The interesting stuff came when he got to the reports written by the investigators doing the secret security clearance. They were required to actually talk to people who knew him and verify different family ties and addresses.

One wrote: Ramon Isaban was born in 1968. His father was an Air Force man who died of a sudden heart attack early in the marriage. Shortly before her husband's death, Maria

Isaban, an immigrant from Spain, gave birth to a baby boy. She named him Ramon Manulito Isaban.

Ramon grew up in Pittsburgh, Pennsylvania. His school transcript indicated average grades. He was said to be a loner and fought often with Anglo boys. One teacher said he seemed to get along better with the minority groups.

Somewhere around the age of fourteen, he began to spend his summers in Spain with relatives and this continued until his graduation from high school.

His visa and passport records verified the above and trips to Spain occurred for four years running with his out-of-country time lasting about three months each summer. After graduation, he returned to Spain for almost one year, again visiting relatives. Further checks made through Naval representatives in Spain confirmed this.

He returned to the U.S. and after six months, joined the Navy. He applied for Aviation Ordnance school while in boot camp, was accepted and completed "A" school with better than average grades. Upon completion of "A" school, he attended Aircraft Munitions school in Oceana, Virginia, Nuclear Weapons loading school in Sanford, Florida, and Nuclear Weapons loading school in Norfolk, Virginia. He then received his orders for assignment to the Venture.

About the only thing that stood out in the background study, the chief thought, was his inability to get along during adolescence and his many trips to visit family in Spain.

The chief thought his appearance was more Arabic than Spanish but then didn't the Moors invade Spain? Maybe he was being too critical. Probably more than half the people in Spain had Moorish blood.

Nevertheless, he said to himself, I think I'll keep an eye on Ramon Manulito Isaban.

15

Ramon forced himself to relax as the chief questioned him about Smitty's little accident. When the questions were finally over, he felt he had handled himself very well and the incident was probably over.

He still regretted having to kill Smitty, not so much because he liked him but because of this very thing now with the chief. He just couldn't risk being exposed. He would, for the sake of Allah complete his assignment, even if it cost him his life. It probably would.

After talking with the chief, he caught up with the crew who were working in a rocket stowage locker. He always enjoyed it when they worked there. All magazines were air-conditioned to keep the explosives stable. The day went by quickly and after evening chow he was lying back on his rack, reading an espionage novel when he heard most everyone's favorite words — mail call.

The crew's first class petty officer walked through the nearby cubicals that were assigned to the hangar deck ordnance crew.

"Black," he called, "Thomas, Redding, Isaban."

Ramon sat up as he heard his name called. The letter came from the only place he ever got mail. He carefully tore the end off, noticing that his hands were shaking a little with anticipation. Pulling out the letter, he began to read.

Dear Ramon,
How are things going for you my son? Could a familyever be closer than we two though we are far apart? Remember under each cloud is a silver lining. Why ever did I talk you into joining the Navy? 8 past midnight and I'm tired. Enough about that. I only have time for a short note but I wanted to let you know that I was thinking of you.
All my love
Your Mom

This time Ramon was more careful. Looking around to assure that no one was looking in his direction, he wrote down the first letter of the first three words of each sentence up to "Enough about that." This time he wrote on his hand so he could wash off the evidence. He noticed two of the words ran together which indicated circling the first letter of the second word as well.

Hat/Cafe/Rue/Wed/8pm

Today was Sunday, the ship would be pulling into port tomorrow. He had to make sure he had liberty on Wednesday. That wouldn't be a problem.

When a guy wanted off on a certain day he could usually trade days with someone else. It was done all the time. Wednesday at eight, he would find out what was going on.

Folding the letter in half, he carefully tore it into many pieces. He crawled to the foot of his bed and, leaning over the foot of his rack, he dropped the shreds into the trash can. He realized that his heart was pounding. He wouldn't be able to sleep until he knew what was going on.

There wasn't a thing he could do until Wednesday.

16

July 19, Venture returns to Cannes.

Tom Barnes stared through the big lenses of the high powered field glasses. He easily overviewed the bay from the third floor apartment they had chosen as their base of operations. The water was very calm and the reflection mirrored the buildings that stood nearest the water. The sun was bright making it easy to see all the early morning activity as Cannes came awake. Scanning Bikini Beach, Tom noticed a few of the early starters arriving for a day of hot sun and picture taking in their quest to make the right contact on the road to stardom. The field glasses paused over the topless ones.

The fishing boats had already left harbor at daylight leaving a large hole in that section of the pier area. The yacht area would remain motionless as the rich dreamed on until a respectable hour to arise. Moving the glasses upward and out into the middle of the bay Tom could see the outline of the super carrier as it completely filled the lenses.

He watched as the Venture dropped anchor. The ship had been out for ten days and a lot can happen in ten days. He was anxious to hear from Matt Blackthorn.

The whole ball game was about to change. Venture was at the end of its six month deployment in the Mediterranean and normally would have returned to its Naval Operations Base at Norfolk, Virginia.

Tom had already sent Frank to set up their new task force headquarters there. Lieutenant Curtis had, however, just received a message from the Department of the Navy, that would change all of that.

The gist of the message was that the President felt, along with Congress, that due to the instability of the world situation, the United States of America needed to provide a morale booster for the world — a demonstration to remind those nations that were supportive of a democratic way of life, that big brother could be there if needed — and quickly. A demonstration to exhibit the tremendous power of the U.S. It was also the general consensus that those countries that chose to view it as threatening could do so.

As a demonstration of its fantastic capabilities, the Venture, upon being relieved of its watch in the Mediterranean, would be escorted by two nuclear powered guided missile ships on a circumnavigation of the globe.

It would be a conclusive demonstration of the special global mobility and self-sufficiency of nuclear powered surface ships.

It *could* be a disaster, Tom Barnes thought, as he heard the news. With the information his department had been handed by British Intelligence how could the Navy possibly plan anything substantial until this deep cover terrorist was apprehended? Lowering the field glasses and taking out his handkerchief, Tom began dabbing his shiny spot.

"Lieutenant, are those gentlemen in Washington aware of the situation we have here?" he asked.

"Yes sir," Lee said. "I tried to impress on them that we need more time. They feel that we've had sufficient time to come up with something and that the whole thing is just a hoax. From what I gather," she said, "they haven't told the President yet."

"God protect us from our leaders," Tom replied.

"The news isn't official yet," said Lee. "The captain of the Venture knows but won't be announcing it until the ship leaves harbor to rendezvous with the relief carrier. That's about a week from now. We have until then to produce. After that, who knows?"

About an hour later, Matt arrived at Lee's apartment. Everyone there anxiously awaited his news. Matt filled them in on what had occurred over the last ten days.

"I've been all over the ship but I swear I can't find a thing that looks suspicious. I've checked the reactor spaces and all critical spaces that we previously selected. There was one thing though."

"What was that? " Tom asked.

"I don't know if it's anything but most of the sailors on that ship usually work in one assigned area. It's unusual to see any one person in a lot of areas but — funny thing — I kept seeing this chief every where I went. It could be legitimate. I heard that the captain ordered a ship-wide security check and the assignment was given to this chief. He is the chief master-at-arms so he's probably okay. Other than that, not a thing," Matt concluded.

"This is frustrating as hell," Tom said, throwing up his hands. "Matt, the only thing we can advise you to do is to continue with the routine but be watchful, something is going to happen and you've got to be ready," he said.

17

Ahmad Hassan stood in the shade of the apartment building across the street from the American lieutenant's apartment.

Ahmad was about five foot two inches and might weigh one hundred and forty pounds wet, but for his size, there wasn't a more feared terrorist cell leader. He was casually dressed in French attire. His black beret was tilted to one side and a large maroon scarf was tied around his neck. His mustache curled upward ever so slightly. He appeared in perfect harmony with his surroundings.

He, of course, knew this as he had been expertly trained over the years to blend into any situation. He had succeeded in many missions in the past and was considered by the Shiite Assassins terrorist planning committee as the best.

Unlike many of his men, he was fanatic about cleanliness. He shaved everyday and believed that to travel among his enemy, he must blend in. He kept himself in good physical condition. He demanded that all of his group remain in top physical condition as well.

His hair was pitch black and he wore it combed back slick on the sides. With his olive skin he could easily pass for Italian, Spanish, Greek or most any Mediterranean nationality.

His long hooked nose gave him an almost evil appearance — an advantage in controlling his men. Ahmad was an absolute expert with a stiletto knife and greatly feared by his men. This expertise had been aptly demonstrated on more than one reluctant group member. When he said move, they moved!

Looking now across the street at the apartment, Hassan realized how long he had waited there — ten days. Although he didn't have to worry about missing what was going on up there. He could easily find out later when he listened to the tapes. His group had monitored the apartment electronically for the last week.

It's amazing, he thought, how small the world really is. One of his group of men had recognized Frank Pierce at a cafe near the beach. They had watched him talking to a black man whom they later identified as Tom Barnes. Frank Pierce had killed the assassin's brother in a shootout during an attempt to sabotage a power plant. This man's first request, upon reporting to Ahmad, was to be allowed to kill Pierce. Ahmad couldn't allow it — yet. It would alert the French police to their presence. Undoubtedly, the French already knew of the Crisis Intervention Group's mission. No, Ahmad's men would have to be patient.

They had very quietly bugged the lieutenant's apartment and, renting another nearby to operate from, they had overheard enough to know the National Security Council was aware of the deep sleeper aboard the Venture. After a week of monitoring, he also knew that was all they knew.

Ahmad was standing here today to get a look at this Matt Blackthorn. Matt was the only one of the group as yet unidentified. He was also the one that must be dealt with to prevent any interference with the operation. It had taken years to plant Ramon in the right spot and he wasn't about to let some meddling sailor disrupt things.

He watched Blackthorn get out of the taxi. While Matt paid for the cab, Ahmad had taken some excellent close ups with his telephoto lens. He then returned to their cover apartment to listen to the operative's conversation.

Stopping at the door to the Assassin's apartment, he knocked rapidly two times then once more. The door opened and he entered just in time to overhear the schedule for the nuclear task force of ships that were about to circle the globe.

"What is this they are saying?" he asked one of his men who was listening.

"The infidel government is sending the Venture and some other ships around the world as a warning to all nations of their power," said the man.

As they listened, they heard Lieutenant Curtis saying, "Matt, you must appear surprised when you hear the captain announce the plan for the world cruise. According to what we've been told, this is the itinerary.

"After leaving the Mediterranean, the task force is to proceed with the circumnavigation by way of Rabat, Morocco; Dakar, Senegal; Freetown, Sierra Leone; Monrovia, Liberia . . ."

She continued listing the various countries they would pass. Only three port calls were scheduled during the cruise. The rest of the places mentioned would have brief visits by "Ambassadors" of the ship. According to the plan, political and military leaders of these countries would be flown aboard.

At each country an airshow would demonstrate the might of the Venture's air power. During the airpower display, air-to-surface and air-to-air missiles like the famous sidewinder were to be demonstrated. Most of the Navy's arsenal would be displayed. There would be demonstrations of various bombing techniques, displays of the aircraft cannons, and other state-of-the-art weaponry.

The visiting leaders of each country would be wined and dined aboard the carrier. This would be the routine at each of the selected countries including the visited ports. The port calls for the Venture were to occur at Karachi, West Pakistan; Sydney, Australia; and Rio De Janeiro, Brazil.

The Venture was to complete the circumnavigation with a widely publicized arrival at New York harbor. Plans included a large celebration with quite a few political figures present, perhaps even the President of the United States.

The goal of the celebration was to stir up public sentiment for the Navy, to the same level that was displayed by the return of The Great White Fleet. Only once previously had a similar role been assigned to ships of the United States Navy when, some eighty-five years before, sixteen first line battleships were sent around the world to test their capabilities and to attract international attention to the range and modern design of American seapower. Those ships had sailed forty-six thousand miles in fourteen months.

This cruise would range thirty-one thousand miles and take sixty-five days.

An evil smile spread over Ahmad Hassan's face. This is incredible, he thought. What more could he ask? When the tapes got back home he would become a permanent member of the planning committee.

Ahmad rubbed his hands together greedily. This information only enhanced their present operation. It allowed them a choice of multiple locations for an incident. There was nothing better in the strategy of terrorism than being able to strike the blow at the precise time and place of their own choosing.

This could be the greatest opportunity to strike a blow for Islam that has ever occurred, he thought. He was elated.

Things began to quiet down at the lieutenant's apartment. It appeared the Americans had completed their briefing of the sailor Blackthorn. Ahmad sent one of his men out to pick up some food. They hated the food in France. These people must put everything they can find in their food, they complained.

The day drifted by slowly. Looking at his watch he took note of the time.

"Continue to monitor the conversation," he ordered, "and take absolutely no action without my permission. Is that understood, Abu?" he said, looking harshly at the man who wanted so badly to kill Frank Pierce.

Abu sat on the floor leaning against the wall. He was an experienced terrorist and had accompanied Ahmad on several missions. He was probably the most fanatic of the group although all his men showed great dedication. Abu always seemed to be the one that started the prayer period and he was the most bitter toward the Americans due to the incident which cost his brother's life.

"As you wish," Abu replied, "but by the will of Allah, I will kill that man. I swear it on the Koran!"

Looking at him, Ahmad knew he meant it. He only hoped he could keep the mad dog on a leash long enough to accomplish their mission.

He had an appointment to keep and he didn't want to be late. This was a very important appointment — the beginning of the greatest operation in the history of the Shiite Assassins.

It was about 7:50 p.m. when he arrived at the Cafe Rue. Several sailors sat at a table near the door. Continuing past them he scanned the place and noticed a sailor sitting at the bar by himself. Casually sitting down by the sailor, he ordered a drink. As the bartender prepared it, Ahmad carefully looked the sailor over. He was about five foot eight inches tall. Black hair and heavy black eyebrows. He felt a great warmth as he took in his fellow countryman. He nodded to the young man and made some comment about the weather. He hoped the sailor noticed his similarity.

"Excuse me," Ahmad said, "could you tell me the time?"

"Sure," Ramon said, looking at his watch. "It's exactly eight p.m."

"Are you off that big ship in the harbor?" Ahmad asked.

"Yes, the Venture," he replied. "By the way," he said holding out his hand, "the name is Ramon. Ramon Isaban."

"Hi, Ramon," Ahmad replied, "My name is Joseph, but you can call me . . . Mr. Hat."

18

Chief Zabrinski sat at a table near the door of the Cafe Rue. He had invited himself to join a couple of other sailors having drinks. He ordered coffee. He saw Ramon sitting at the bar alone.

It was easy to follow Ramon. If he was a terrorist, he sure was a careless one. He never once looked back to see if anyone was following.

Zabrinski had been in the same liberty launch and hoped that Ramon wouldn't notice him. Ramon didn't even look up during the ride. He seemed preoccupied with other things.

He had, in fact, followed Ramon pretty closely for the past several days. He probably wouldn't have been sitting here at the Cafe Rue right now if he hadn't witnessed the previous evening's incident.

After the evening meal at the chief's mess, he had retired to his compartment. He had undressed, and wrapping a towel around himself, was about to head for the showers. It suddenly dawned on him that most of the crew was involved in the same routine.

This gave him the idea to take advantage of the situation and do a little spying of his own. Grabbing his shaving gear, the chief left his compartment and walked only a short distance down the passageway to the ladder of the G Division compartment. Before his assignment to the master-at-arms office, the chief had worked with this department, as his rating was Aviation Ordnance.

Most of the younger men in the division had never worked with Zabrinski as he had been the chief master-at-arms for several years. Walking across the compartment in his towel with his shaving kit brought no attention whatsoever. He wanted to get as close to Ramon's cubical as possible. Suddenly he came upon an E-5 that knew him from the past.

"Chief Zabrinski," said the petty officer, "what brings you down to this neck of the woods?"

"How are you doing, Ron?" he replied. "Oh we're having a bit of trouble in the showers at the chief's compartment so I thought since yours was close you wouldn't mind."

Looking toward Ramon's cubical, he could see a petty officer handing out some mail.

"Looks like you guys have been pretty busy lately," the chief commented.

"Boy you can say that again. We've been bustin' our butts, Chief," he replied.

Ramon had sat up on his rack and was reading the letter that was given him. He appeared totally engrossed.

"Chief," Ron said, "did you hear that we on-reped over three hundred and fifty tons of ordnance the other day? We got the stuff coming out our ears down in the magazines."

Ramon now reached into his locker, pulled out a pen and

then looked around. The chief turned his head a little, hoping he hadn't been noticed.

"You wouldn't happen to have any skinny you could let us in on concerning this larger than normal inventory, would you Chief?" he was asked.

Looking up, the chief saw Ramon writing something on his hand. He looked back at the letter and then repeated the process several times.

"Your guess is as good as mine," Zabrinski responded. "One thing's for sure, you can bet the captain knows and when it strikes his fancy, I'm sure we'll be let in on the secret."

Now Ramon was tearing up the letter. Crawling to the foot of his rack, he leaned over the edge and dropped the remnants into the trash can.

The chief visited a bit longer and pretended to head for the showers. He turned back, retracing his path to make sure Ramon didn't notice him.

When taps sounded that evening, the chief was standing on the hangar deck talking to Johnson.

"What's up, Chief?" Johnson asked, out of breath. "I hauled ass up here as fast as I could."

"I have a little job for you Jack. I want you to follow me through the G Division compartment and when I indicate by pointing at a certain trash can, you make a mental note of it. Make yourself inconspicuous until everyone is asleep. When you're sure everything is quiet, take the can I have indicated, up on the mess decks and find another to replace it. Make sure the replacement can has trash in it. Then bring the can in question up to my office. Don't lose sight of that can once I point it out and don't be seen," he ordered.

"Wow, Chief, this sounds like cloak and dagger stuff. Do you want to let me in on it?"

"When I can, Jack," Zabrinski said. "Please bear with me until then."

"Sure Chief, whatever you say," Johnson replied with a perplexed look.

At about midnight, Johnson showed up with the trash can. The two of them spent about fifteen minutes picking out all the torn pieces of the letter.

The chief dismissed Johnson, reminding him this was between the two of them. Zabrinski began to tape the pieces back together. Ramon had torn up the letter quite effectively and it took the chief two hours to reassemble it.

Looking at the results, it appeared to be a normal letter from a mother to her son. A couple of places in the letter seemed unusual. She appeared to start off several of the sentences strangely like, "Could a family ever be closer than we two."

Most people would say "How could a family ever be closer than we two?"

In another example he found, "Remember under each dark cloud is a silver lining."

That seemed somewhat out of context. He couldn't put his finger on it.

He tried writing the missing words down. That didn't make any sense. Then he tried looking for an esoteric meaning to the sentences. Again — nothing.

Next he tried selecting various words and putting them together to assemble something. Every other word, every fourth word, then he tried the whole sequence backwards. Still nothing.

He was tired. It was about zero three-thirty and he was willing to accept defeat when one last idea occurred to him. He hadn't tried various letter combinations to make up words yet.

Another hour passed and he had something. He could only assume what most of it meant but by taking the first letter of the first three words of each sentence, he could at least understand some of the words.

Hat - Caf - Rue - Wed - 8pm - Eat - Ioh

He knew he had the terrorist for sure now, but would the letter be proof enough?

He was brought back to the present in the Cafe Rue by a voice in the distance.

"I'd bet you would too, wouldn't you Chief?"

"What's that?" he replied to the joking sailor.

"We were just saying how a little action might be in order, if you know what I mean. How about it, Chief, are you with us?"

"Well thanks for the invitation, gentlemen, but some other time perhaps," he replied. "I think there will be some action here eventually."

"Here?" said the other sailor. "This place is like a morgue."

"Well, we're out of here," they both said in unison as they drained their glasses. Leaving a fist full of francs, they bade the chief farewell.

Zabrinski picked up his coffee and casually moved a bit closer to the bar. He had seen the man come in and sit beside Ramon. He wanted to pick up some of the conversation if at all possible. He had just sat down when he heard the man introducing himself.

"Hi, Ramon, my name is Joseph, but you can call me . . . Mr. Hat."

19

"Leave in five minutes," said Ahmad. "A green Peugeot will stop for you out front."

With that, Ahmad got up and walked out.

Ramon could hardly wait the five minutes. Staring at himself in the mirror behind the bar he thought back to the many times he had pondered the future— the thousands of questions he had asked himself like — when the time comes will I be able to sacrifice myself for Islam?

He knew he would attempt to do whatever was expected of him, he just hoped he wouldn't fail. This was a much bigger thing than a military action. It was an affirmation of what God expected.

His heart picked up its pace as he paid the tab, and walked out in front of the Cafe Rue. A green Peugeot roared from the shadows of the unlit street, sliding to a stop in front of him.

Its door swung open, beckoning him. As he stepped in he was thrown against the seat as it accelerated away from the curb.

The chief ran outside and watched the Peugeot scream away. Looking up and down the street he realized there wasn't a taxi in sight. He had lost Ramon and his . . . Mr. Hat.

As the car sped away from the cafe, Ahmad turned to Ramon and said, "Allah be blessed. A new day is beginning and a sleeping warrior awakened. Welcome to the war, my brother!"

"I can't explain how pleased I am," Ramon said. "I have waited long."

Ahmad drove Ramon across Cannes as hastily as possible. Undue attention was out of the question. He turned frequently, always keeping to the side streets and even doubling back on two occasions to assure they weren't being followed. Ramon observed and asked no questions, knowing full well all would be disclosed soon enough.

The journey took them to the outskirts of the city. As the lights began to fade they drove down a long dirt road into a farming community. The road was lined with very large trees which cast long shadows by the full moon. The smell of alfalfa was heavy on the night air. Turning into a lane, the car sped toward a small cottage some distance from the road. The Peugeot slid to a stop near a door which led from the side of the cottage to the driveway. Ahmad turned and, looking at Ramon, said jokingly, "This is what you might call our local training center."

They got out of the car and approached the door to the cottage. It opened automatically by a very large man with a beard. He held a Russian built AK 47 assault rifle.

Ramon was quite familiar with the weapon. He had fired it many times in training. He actually preferred it over its American counterpart, the M-16, which often jammed at the most inopportune times.

"So, this is our valiant sleeper," the man said stepping forward and surrounding Ramon with a bear hug.

"Meet Asam, Ramon, my most trusted brother," Ahmad added.

Asam stepped back and bowed, looking Ramon over curiously. He was one of the largest men Ramon had ever seen. The assault rifle looked small in his huge hands. His black hair and beard made him appear very out of place in this land of small thin people. His smile was an obvious door to his heart and Ramon knew this was a man he could trust with his life. This was a true servant of Allah.

"He would look much better if he weren't dressed in the clothes of an infidel!" replied Asam.

"I have interesting news to tell you, Ramon," Ahmad began as they entered the cottage. "Through our local sources, we have discovered that the Venture and two other nuclear powered ships are to depart the Mediterranean shortly to circumnavigate the globe.

"This provides us with many opportunities to create an incident that could greatly embarrass the mighty Eagle. The ship will be departing in about one more week. That doesn't give us sufficient time to enlighten you with the knowledge necessary to accomplish your task but other arrangements will be made."

"What will my task be?" Ramon asked.

"All in good time, my impatient one," Ahmad said. "I realize that you are limited in the number of days that you can leave the ship so we will have to make the best use of the time."

"Take off your jumper and relax," Asam said as he entered the room. He was preceded by the spicy smell of tea. He carried several cups on a tray. "We have only two hours before you must return to the ship."

Closing the curtains, Ahmad and Asam set up a projection screen and a projector.

"Ramon, do you remember a while back there were two U.S. Navy men arrested for espionage?" Ahmad began. "They had been selling U.S. secrets to the Russians. It was very important information concerning the nuclear devices used by the American Navy. We now have in our possession the bulk of that data, and in fact, you will see most of it during your training.

"Our illustrious leaders have, for a very long time, attempted to acquire sufficient radioactive materials to build and test a tactical nuclear weapon. This of course has been extremely difficult. With such a weapon we could truly hold the Western world for ransom."

Asam joined in. "We had facilities constructed in Baghdad and were in the process of testing the components when the invasion of Kuwait took place. When the retaliation from NATO occurred, our test facilities were bombed heavily. Most of the equipment was destroyed along with most of the personnel capable of creating a device.

"The joint NATO nuclear monitoring team now makes it very difficult to continue with the operation. Our leader feels that we have the right to these weapons and with them, we could be in a major bargaining position. He feels that in the past we could have used such weapons, and if we had them, would not be in our present world position."

Ahmad seemed unable to sit still. He paced to the window and back before he spoke.

"You have been awakened just for this purpose. Islam intends to make a major comment to the world through your glorious sacrifice. We realize that it may be difficult, if not impossible, to plan an exact operation due to the nature of the ship's security. It may become necessary for you to take action

at any opportunity. We must therefore enlighten you suffi-
ciently to do so at that opportune moment.

"You are expert in the field of ordnance and are in a good
position for any type of conventional attack, but our leader
wants to send a much greater message to the world. A message
that will be heard in every city of every country on the globe.
A nuclear message!"

Ahmad paused for effect. Ramon found himself holding his
breath.

"At the opportune time of our choice, you will destroy the
largest aircraft carrier in the world. The nuclear powered
U.S.S. Venture!" The air in the room felt heavy, ringing with
the glorious words.

"I realize," said Ahmad, taking a deep breath, "that you do
not have full access to the nuclear components on the ship,
other than some exposure to the nuclear weapons while participating in loading exercises. I also realize that you have no
access whatsoever to the reactors. We of the planning committee are working on several scenarios that would allow you to
take action, no matter what opportunity presents itself."

"This is where the training comes in," Asam said. "You
might also say the time frame as well. Our leader wishes the
action to take place within the next six months while the
world's eyes are still on Iraq.

"Knowing the scheduled stops the Venture will make over
the next few months will enable us to more precisely select a
target location that best benefits our cause. In the meantime,
you must become expert in two other fields.

"One, the inner workings of the nuclear reactors aboard
the Venture and their point of weakness.

"Two, the inner workings of the nuclear *weapons* that are
in the arsenal of the Venture and how to sabotage them."

Ramon looked at the projection screen and his education
began on the various types of reactors and their differences.

In the back of his mind, however, Ahmad's words were still ringing over and over - *YOUR GLORIOUS SACRIFICE!*

The first slide appeared.

1. LWR - light water reactor
2. HWR - heavy-water reactor
3. HTGR - high-temperature gas-cooled reactor
4. LMFBR - liquid-metal fast-breeder reactor

The time ticked by as Ahmad talked on about the reactors, how they functioned and what Ramon might do to create a melt down or other major reaction. He was quite an expert on the subject and had it not been for the situation, Ramon might have imagined himself sitting in a lecture at some university.

Looking at his watch, Ahmad nodded to Asam as he said, "We will continue your education at our next opportunity. Take him back to the ship. He must not be late," Ahmad ordered.

Asam said very little on the way back to the boat landing. As Ramon got out of the car Asam grabbed his arm and Ramon turned to face him.

"Ramon, you are the most important soldier in Islam at this moment. Your burden is greater than that of any holy man. The future of Islam could lie in those small hands. Sleep well, my little brother, but remember you don't sleep alone. You are surrounded by as many prayers as the hairs on a camel."

Then with a huge smile he drove away, leaving Ramon standing alone on the dock.

They had arrived at the pier just in time for the final liberty boat back to the ship. Ramon hurried across the pier. The launch was waiting at the landing, the engine running as it gently rocked back and forth next to the moonlit pier. It was crammed full of the diehard liberty hounds that squeezed every second out of the time allowed away from the ship. There was much cursing and singing as the shore patrol officers assisted the inebriated crewmen aboard.

The ride back to the ship was a time to contemplate and Ramon wondered about what the future had in store for him.

As the launch approached the ship, Ramon looked back at the lights of Cannes. He didn't see a beautiful panoramic scene, the light reflecting off the water, nor the sparkling lights of the buildings, streets, and cars. He couldn't hear the roar of the engine or feel the vibration it created. He was unable to feel the cool evening breeze or the spray of the water as the launch knifed its way to the ship.

To him, everything was overshadowed by a very large cloud . . . with a mushroom shape.

20

"What the hell is going on?" Frank Pierce demanded. The show of temper was completely unlike him. "I just get to Virginia to set up the new ops base, and they haul my butt back to NSC headquarters. Next thing I know, I'm on a plane back here."

"Calm down, Frank," Tom soothed, "I've been ordered by Swager to shut down the place here in Cannes."

"What? They think the danger's over?"

"Not at all," Lee Curtis interrupted. "With Mike Young's death, they believe it more than ever."

"Didn't you hear, Frank? The Venture is pulling out of the Med," Matt added. "We're going on an around-the-world cruise. Of course, the captain hasn't announced it yet."

"I need you here to close up the apartment, Frank," Tom said. "I have to go on ahead."

They all sat around the kitchen table sipping on the strong local coffee.

"I'll never get used to this stuff and I'm sure as hell not gonna miss it," Frank announced.

"Matt," Tom said. "I was reminded . . .," turning, he looked at Lee with a smile, "that you gave up your week of leave time to pitch in and help out with the investigation. As a consolation, I have arranged with your captain for you to have a few days off, beginning today. With the Venture setting sail for the next couple of months, you deserve a break."

Tom instructed him to continue snooping around once they sailed and to report anything suspicious to the captain.

"Lee," Tom continued, "you have been invaluable to us and I hope you will continue to be, but at this point, I have no alternative but to release you back to the Navy. I'll make it official in, let's say, three days. That should give you some time to enjoy the French Riviera. Take advantage of it.

"And by the way," he said, "when we regroup, and we will regroup, you'll be there with us. In fact, you'll probably hear from me sooner that you think."

"Thank you, Tom," she said. "Thank you for everything."

A couple of hours later, Tom was on a big jet somewhere over the Atlantic Ocean. He would continue the investigation from his Washington office for the time being. When Frank joined him, they would put their heads together and come up with a plan.

Ahmad heard the whole conversation. Time was quickly running out in Cannes for Ramon's training. His information source that had been so generously providing them with valuable input, was about to dry up.

The way he saw it, he had a major threat to his operation at the moment. He had to deal with it. This would be a good opportunity.

All he would have to do was follow Matt Blackthorn during his holiday. He was certain that an opportunity would come to get Mr. Blackthorn out of the picture. His thoughts were interrupted by his man operating the monitoring device.

"They are talking again," Abu said. "It sounds like Blackthorn and the woman."

Ahmad took the headset from the man and began to listen.

"Lee," Matt said, "you walked in at the beginning of my leave and led me to believe you were interested in me. Of course, I quickly learned it was business. Well, the business has been put on hold for a while. I find myself with a few days off and so do you. You don't know the Riviera and I do. What say we rent a car and drive up the coast to Nice, and visit Monaco? There's a lot to see and I'd love to share it with you."

There was a pause. She smiled. "I'd like that Matt, I'd like that a lot."

Ahmad thought for a moment about the opportunity. It really wasn't necessary to kill the woman but he had no other choice. If she was in the way when he took out Blackthorn, well, that was the will of Allah. Turning, he began to bark out orders.

"Remove this equipment to the training center and vacate the apartment. I want you to prepare my car, fill it with gas and check that it is ready. Put a well equipped tool box, ten ounces of C4, and several different types of ignitors in the trunk."

There was a pause in his commands and his men all sat there waiting for the next one.

"Immediately!" he screamed, and with that they all jumped to their feet and hurried about to complete the assignment.

As Abu walked past, Ahmad grabbed him by the arm.

"Tomorrow night, after this place has been cleaned up and no trace of our being here remains, you may visit the lieutenant's apartment. Take everything of any value and wreck the place."

"And Frank Pierce?" Abu said, almost like a kid about to get something he has wanted for a long time.

"If he happens to be killed by burglars during a robbery attempt, well, those things happen," Ahmad said with a smile, as he slapped Abu on the shoulder.

The big terrorist grinned with satisfaction. He was beside himself. Allah was good to him and now he would avenge his brother.

An hour later, a taxi stopped in front of the lieutenant's apartment. Lee and Matt climbed inside and it accelerated away from the curb. About one hundred yards in trail, Ahmad followed at the wheel of his green Peugeot. The taxi dropped the couple off at a rental car area and about twenty minutes later a blue Mercedes convertible pulled out onto the street. In it were a young couple with smiles on their faces and not a care in the world.

Still one hundred yards behind, followed Ahmad.

The highway to Nice was a two lane road cut along the cliff with a rock retainer wall on the ocean side and a solid rock wall on the other.

Matt was at the wheel and he and Lee were totally unaware of anything except each other. The little green Peugeot passed them unnoticed.

As the highway began to ascend a hill, the powerful Mercedes soon closed the distance to the Peugeot. The little under-powered green car continued to slow down. Matt slowed as well, restricted by the no passing zone.

They continued to trail the Peugeot as it slowly ascended the hill. The two vehicles now neared the crest of the hill. From his position in the leading vehicle, Ahmad could now see over the hill, and what he saw was a large truck about to crest the hill in the opposite direction.

Ahmad reduced the pressure on the accelerator, bringing the small car to a slow crawl. He carefully judged the distance of the approaching truck. When he thought the timing was right, he put his arm out of the window and motioned for the Mercedes to pass him.

Matt, thinking the driver of the Peugeot was giving him the all clear, accelerated to pass. As he came alongside the Peugeot, it suddenly began to accelerate as well.

A moment later the truck crested the hill and Matt and Lee found themselves face to face with the oncoming giant. Matt couldn't swerve to the right due to Ahmad's carefully positioned Peugeot. The left was obviously blocked by the solid rock embankment.

Matt reacted automatically, slamming on the brake pedal and jerking the wheel hard to the right. The Mercedes responded nicely as it once again fell in behind the Peugeot.

The truck missed the left front fender of the Mercedes by inches. The sound of the truck's horn accompanied by a deluge of French curse words faded with the distance.

"Shit! That was close!" Matt breathed.

"Yeah, what the hell happened? I'd swear that Peugeot just set us up!" Lee added, her eyes wide.

Once they crested the hill, Matt could see the road was clear ahead and he accelerated around the little green car. As they passed, both Matt and Lee stared at the crazy man who'd almost killed them. The driver responded with a lazy shrug of his shoulders.

Not far down the road, Matt pulled into a roadside cafe. Lee drank two cups of espresso before she stopped shaking. In another twenty minutes they resumed their journey, putting the unpleasant experience behind them. They were determined not to let anything spoil their holiday. Not too far behind, Ahmad followed, staying just out of sight. He was angry at his failure and already looking for another opportunity.

The two continued their drive up the winding road along the coast. The view was spectacular and the weather couldn't have been better.

Arriving in Nice in the afternoon, they drove along the Promenade des Anglais. The beautiful boulevard was lined with tall palm trees. It bordered the sea on one side, and was lined with the most luxurious hotels and mansions on the other. Lee had called before leaving Cannes and made reservations at the Hotel Beach Regency. It was located right on the Promenade des Anglais and they soon spotted it.

They parked the car in the front parking lot and found their way to the lobby. As they arrived at the reception desk, the clerk greeted them with a smile saying, "Yes, may I help you?"

"We have a reservation," Lee replied. "It's under the name Lee Curtis."

"Yes, here we have it," the clerk replied, "Lee Curtis, small suite for two, balcony view of the ocean, and let's see, ah yes, king size bed."

Matt looked at Lee, a bit surprised. Smiling at him, she began to blush.

"Keep that bloom in your cheeks," he said, "it looks good on you."

A bellhop, who didn't stop grinning the entire time, escorted them to their room. He showed them around the suite, indicating the bathroom and opening the doors to the balcony for them.

"Is romantical view for lovers," he said in his broken English.

Ahmad sat in the parking lot waiting to plan his next move. As he looked at the face of the building he saw Matt and Lee walk out on the balcony of a room on the third floor.

"How convenient," he said out loud. "You've saved me a lot of foot work."

Leaning back in the seat he prepared himself for the long wait.

It wasn't as long as he anticipated. Glancing up at their room, he noticed the doors were closed again. He was about to get out of the car to insure they were still there when Matt and Lee emerged from the hotel lobby. They proceeded to their car and drove out into the traffic. He followed.

Driving through the old town of Nice, which was a busy little port, they slowed to enjoy the scenery. The streets were winding, steep and narrow, lined with tall houses with balconies on which laundry and flower pots competed for space.

In each busy square they passed, the many flower markets exploded in rainbows of colors. Continuing up the road they entered the Principality of Monaco.

They were definitely determined to enjoy themselves, thought Ahmad.

In Monte Carlo, they drove up to the buff-colored, fortress-like palace of Prince Ranier, the reigning sovereign of the state. Parking the car, the two strolled arm in arm in front of the castle.

Remaining out of sight, Ahmad walked along behind them reading the information about the palace and pretending interest. The palace had occupied that spot since the thirteenth century. It was built on a rocky spur which juts out into the sea, surrounded on three sides by cliffs with a sheer drop to the water. He wished they would take an interest in viewing the cliffs. They didn't.

He followed them next to the Casino of Monte Carlo where they walked around outside viewing the gardens.

Finally, they returned to the hotel. He sat in the Peugeot watching their room. Shortly, the doors opened to the balcony and this was what he had been waiting for. He knew they would be occupied for a while.

This gave him the opportunity to get something to eat. He walked across the street to a nearby cafe. He selected a table that allowed him to see their balcony doors from his seat. The menu offered only French food, but he was hungry. He ate for the first time that day. Afterward, he purchased several magazines, returned to his car, and settled in for the wait.

It was around midnight when the lights in their room finally went out. He continued to wait until all was quiet and most of the people enjoying the area had called it a night.

Looking at his watch, it was three ten. The parking lot lights illuminated most of the lot very well. Too well, he thought.

Starting his car, he moved the Peugeot to a place near the Mercedes. Getting out of the Peugeot, he walked over to the base of the light that loomed just above the Mercedes. Several well aimed stones eventually paid off as the light burst. Looking around, he checked to see if the noise of the shattering light had attracted any attention. The parking lot was still empty.

In a short time he had opened the hood on the Mercedes. Removing the tool box that one of his men had placed in the Peugeot, he selected an adjustable wrench. Holding a small flashlight in his mouth, he quickly removed the fuel line where it entered the fuel injection system. Taking a small file, he filed the threads off both sides of the connection. Next, he slid the fitting back on and wrapped exactly two turns of electrical tape around the junction.

He then taped a pull-type ignitor, which was normally used to ignite a fuse for explosives, to the fuel injector housing. He also taped the pull-ring of the ignitor to the fuel line.

He estimated that the Mercedes would run for about thirty minutes before the pressure of the fuel would push the fuel line rearward causing a small fuel leak. This would soften the tape holding the fuel line to the fuel injector housing. Shortly thereafter the tape would suddenly let go and as the fuel line separated from the housing, it would spray fuel all over the inside of the engine while simultaneously the pull ring would be drawn through the ignitor, igniting the fuel-air mixture. The ignitor he selected had a one minute delay. That would give sufficient time for enough fuel to be dispersed to create a good explosive potential.

Normally it would only cause a good engine fire and without oxygen it wouldn't burn well at all. He couldn't depend on Blackthorn to open the hood however, so to assure the explosion, he had taped a heat sensitive blasting cap around the ignitor.

He hated make-shift bombs. Sometimes they worked and sometimes, they didn't. He wished he could use the C-4 explosive. It always did the job and would have been much easier but that would bring in all kinds of police. That could cause problems in getting out of the country over the next few weeks. He and his men had to leave very shortly so an accident was the best approach.

Quietly, he closed the hood of the Mercedes. Looking around, he insured that everything appeared as before. Putting the flashlight, tape and wrench back in the tool box, he set it back in the trunk of the Peugeot and, climbing in, drove out of the parking lot to return to Cannes.

"One less problem for my sleeping sailor," he said, leaving Nice.

21

July 20th.

Ramon had liberty and was one of the first men off the ship that morning. Climbing off the liberty launch, he hurried down the pier to the nearest telephone booth and dialed the number given him by Ahmad. Using the assigned password to identify himself, he gave his location. He was advised to proceed to the main avenue where he would be picked up.

Hanging up, he left the phone booth and proceeded up the street toward the main avenue about two blocks away. Standing on the curb he waited. Shortly, the little green Peugeot pulled up in front of him. Ahmad sat at the wheel.

"I've been waiting for you," he said with a smile.

Ahmad pulled into the busy traffic and they continued up the main avenue. As on his previous ride to the cottage,

Ramon noticed how Ahmad drove his zig-zag course to throw off anyone that might be following. He even made a U-turn at one intersection and retraced their route for about a block. Making another U-turn, they continued on the original route.

"We can't be too careful," Ahmad told him.

In about twenty minutes they were turning onto the lane that led up to the cottage.

Just as they came to a stop in the driveway, the door to the cottage opened and Asam appeared. He opened the car door for Ramon.

"Welcome, little brother," he said smiling.

Ramon liked Asam.

It's funny, he thought, we're working together, we believe in the same cause and we might even die together. Yet, I don't know a single personal thing about this man.

As they entered the cottage Ahmad pointed to a chair.

"You must make yourself comfortable, and we will begin."

Ahmad was quite knowledgeable and well prepared for the instruction with slides and diagrams. It soon became apparent to Ramon that this wasn't a hastily planned operation but had probably been in the works for years. Ahmad had become expert in the subjects, specifically to teach Ramon.

Ahmad reviewed the types of reactors discussed in the last lesson and was beginning a more thorough explanation.

"The nuclear reactor, Ramon, is a device in which the fission reaction involving neutrons and nuclear fuels is controlled for the production of heat energy.

"As you know, the heat energy is converted through the use of turbines and generators to horsepower for the screws of the Venture as well as its other energy needs." He dimmed the lights and switched on the projector.

"The essential components of a reactor are first, the fuel, which may be natural uranium, enriched uranium or highly enriched uranium.

"Second, a moderator in the form of ordinary water, heavy water, graphite, beryllium, or BeO to slow down the neutrons produced during fission so that they can be captured by fuel nuclei.

"And, thirdly, coolant, in the form of water, heavy water, helium gas, carbon dioxide, air, or liquid sodium etc, to extract fission heat for useful purposes." He pointed to diagrams on the projection screen. Ramon listened intently.

"If the amount of fuel brought together in one place is too small, with a large surface-to-volume ratio, neutron leakage from the mass is excessive, and the system is termed *subcritical*. When enough material has been accumulated that one neutron gives rise to the production of exactly one additional neutron, the system is termed *critical* and is said to have reached *critical mass*. A mass in excess of this will result in what is called the *supercritical* condition and will exhibit a growth in the number of neutrons.

"The power of the reactor will depend upon the neutron population and the amount of fissile material. The operation of the reactor is controlled by the adjustment of neutron absorbers, usually consisting of a boron compound in solution, and control rods, which are made of boron or cadmium.

"The neutron multiplication factor of the reactor is maintained at 1.0 for steady operation and is decreased or increased slightly to effect a drop or rise in power.

"As the nuclear fuel is consumed, the absorption must be reduced to maintain the critical state and this may be done by diluting the boron solution. Eventually, all control is removed, and the reactor must be shut down to replace some fuel. That's the basics of a reactor and how it's controlled, Ramon."

Ramon felt his head swimming with details. He blinked to restore his concentration.

"Continuing," Ahmad said, "the Venture is equipped with eight heavy-water reactors (HWR). These use natural uranium as fuel, heavy water as the moderator, and ordinary water as the coolant. This type has the advantage of not requiring an enrichment process.

"To prevent overheating of the fuel rods, reactors are designed with safety devices to keep the power below a specified level. If the power for any reason exceeds this level, neutron-absorbing control rods are inserted automatically. The power drops from its operating value to a much lower value, which corresponds to the delayed effects of fission. This latter value, is called the afterheat and declines slowly over months. Pumps circulate fuel-cooling water through a closed loop designed for low leakage.

"If excess leakage is sensed, a separate high-pressure injection pump transfers stored water to the reactor vessel. Additional water from a second tank is then forced into the reactor core by the use of compressed nitrogen gas. Valves are closed to prevent radioactive liquid and gas from escaping from the containment building, in this case the reactor spaces of the Venture."

Ahmad produced more slides that showed the various parts of the reactor and its components. Ramon began to understand it better and they discussed the weak and strong points for hours.

A course eventually became apparent in which a reactor could be made to melt down, which could possibly cause an explosion and at the very least would create contamination that would require years to clean up.

Ahmad disclosed at this point the plan that had been prepared by the committee.

"If a valve that allows the supply of feed-water to the steam generator were to be closed during operation, the generator would rapidly boil dry and thus could not remove the decay heat from the reactor core, this would cause an increase in temperature and pressure in the primary cooling system.

"If the pressurizer relief valve *somehow* became stuck open, this would allow a considerable amount of cooling water to escape from the reactor vessel. Due to the temperature of the water, it would be automatically pumped to an auxiliary holding tank. The emergency core-cooling system would begin to make up water loss but would be misinterpreted by the operators who would shut off the ECCS or the emergency cooling control system and the main coolant pump as well.

"This action would lead to the uncovering of the core and, because it would no longer be surrounded by cooling water, the core would heat up and core melting would occur. This would result in a core melt down, the results of which could be catastrophic both for the Venture and a surrounding area of approximately one hundred miles."

Ramon was stunned. He had imagined using explosive devices capable of killing twenty or thirty people at a time, at the most. With the exception of the bombing of the Pan Am flight, most terrorist activities were limited to killing smaller groups of people. The world attention brought about by the bombing of flight 103 was a perfect example of the negative attention brought to Islam by the destruction of a large group of people.

He couldn't fathom such an operation. If this were successful, over five thousand people aboard the ship alone would be killed. If the location of the action took place in a densely populated area, no telling how many more thousands would be killed outright or die in the following years from radiation poisoning.

"Ahmad, may I say something?" he asked.

Ahmad nodded in consent.

"I'm sure that you and the members of the Committee have considered the absolute catastrophic consequences of an action on a level of this proportion." he began nervously.

"Perhaps, Ahmad, you would help me to understand how

this will help Islam. Have you considered that such an act is so vile and unacceptable to the infidel, that . . . well . . . that all the other religions might unite to turn against the nation of Islam. Can we risk such a great gamble?"

Ahmad paused for a moment as if looking for the right words, then calmly, he began.

"When the atomic bomb was dropped on Hiroshima, over seventy-eight thousand people were killed outright. The bodies of about ten thousand were never found — probably vaporized. Did the world unite against the United States? Shortly after that, when the bomb intended for a target near Nagasaki missed its mark and destroyed half the city killing forty thousand people, did the world unite against the United States? When the Turks slaughtered close to one million Armenians, during the First World War, did the world unite against them? When the Russians attempted genocide against the Jews at the turn of the century, did the world unite against them?

"In order to control an army, a general often makes an example of several soldiers and in some cases several thousand. With few exceptions, nothing is ever done to them.

"The same is true of countries. In Japan, during the period of the war-lords and shoguns, the two major armies of the land would meet in a great decisive battle. The battle might rage for days and even weeks and when it was over and a truce was called, the moment the defeated army surrendered, the head of every single man of the defeated army would be chopped off. This was done because trust could never be extended to the losers. They fought their battles and risked their lives for allegiance to one man.

"The United States places its allegiance in democracy, its materialistic way of life. England places its values on the Monarchy and what it represents. Islam places its allegiance in Allah!"

"Why do you think the hundreds of thousands of people of Islam are so dedicated to their religion? Because not to fear Allah is to commit suicide. There is no middle ground. There is but one choice - Allah!

"We are the soldiers of Allah, Ramon. He sends his blessings to those that believe through the sweet words of the Koran. He sends his vengeance to those that don't through his army of soldiers. You will have the privilege of delivering that message, Ramon. Our intention is genocide of all infidels. They will become true believers or they will not be — at all! "

Ahmad's eyes glowed with fervor. His strong nose became even more prominent. Ramon felt a chill touch his neck.

"Our message is not meant for those men who will die. It is meant for all those that will continue. It's to shock them to their senses. This can't be accomplished by filing a complaint with the United Nations.

"What is the meaning of a few thousand American sailors in comparison with the millions that might join us when they realize how mighty Allah really is!

"You must shout as loud as you can, Ramon so your message will carry all the way around the world!" he concluded.

Ramon understood now how insignificant his concern truly was. His mother's words came back to him — and the sting of leather against his back. He understood now and felt his total dedication growing in him, overwhelming him with pride in Islam.

"Forgive my stupidity, my brother. I have lived with the infidels for so long that I have begun to think like one. You have opened my eyes to my error. May the will of Allah prevail! Help me to achieve success for Islam!"

Suddenly Asam picked up the AK-47 assault rifle and, quickly aiming in Ramon's direction, pulled the trigger.

22

Chief Zabrinski was ready for Ramon this time. He was convinced that Ramon was the man he was after. Ramon had probably killed Mike Young, he thought, because he recognized him from some previous encounter of the past. Smith was probably just an unfortunate victim that was killed because of something he might have seen or heard.

He couldn't very well march Ramon up to the captain and say, "Here is your terrorist."

Ramon would only reply, "I don't know what he is talking about, sir. You can check my record and you will see it is spotless and has been for years."

He could see it all unfolding. "Well what about the letter the chief has here that you tore up and threw in the trash?" the captain would say.

"What letter?" Ramon would reply.

"This letter," the chief would say. "See here it says Dear Ramon."

Ramon could easily say he had never seen that particular letter in his life. Legally speaking, since the chief had left the compartment, thereby losing sight of the trash can, he couldn't prove that this was the exact letter Ramon had torn up and thrown away.

It would be his word against Ramon's. No, there wasn't enough evidence, yet. He had to know what Ramon was up to. He had to catch him with enough evidence to prove his involvement in whatever it was that he was planning. He had to be caught in the act and there must be other witnesses and more tangible proof. Then this filthy traitor could be locked up where he belonged.

They watched as Ramon got off the liberty launch and walked down the pier to a public phone booth. He made a call, left the booth and proceeded up the street that met the pier. He walked about four blocks to the intersection of the main avenue.

Their small rented car followed slowly, keeping Ramon in sight but prepared to pull over as if to park, at any indication of suspicion on Ramon's part.

Yes the chief was prepared this time. He wasn't about to let Ramon go zipping off in a taxi while he stood there twiddling his thumbs. He had also brought a little help in the form of the gunnery sergeant of the Marine detachment that was stationed on the Venture.

Sergeant Bond had served aboard the Venture for about as long as Chief Zabrinski. They were not only good friends but often worked together in matters pertaining to prisoners. Gunny as he was called, was in charge of the brig.

Gunny was a six foot tall, one hundred and ninety pound chunk of combat solider. There wasn't a crease in his uniform that wasn't supposed to be there. He set the example which was held so proudly by the Marine Corps. He had served in Vietnam with distinction and was one of those kind of men that the officers consulted, rather than the other way around.

The chief, due to his restrictive orders, had not confided in the gunny, but had only told him he would appreciate his company. He did explain that it was a matter of security concerning the Venture, and that the captain was aware of it. That was good enough for the gunny.

Security was his job aboard the Venture. He not only ran the brig but his company of Marines also ran the security system and sentry posts that controlled access to the nuclear weapons spaces. The chief had told him to bring a pistol and he had armed himself with a standard issue Colt .45 automatic.

"I assume we're following someone, Chief?" he asked after observing the snail's pace of their car.

"That's right, Gunny, one of those sailors about a block ahead, and when we get the opportunity without exposing ourselves, I'll point him out to you."

Ramon had stopped and seemed to be looking up and down the road. The chief pulled over to the curb about a block from Ramon and waited.

A green Peugeot pulled up to the curb, Ramon jumped in, and it sped off.

"That's what we've been waiting for, Gunny," he said as he stepped hard on the accelerator. The rental car jumped into the traffic with a screech of rubber and the sound of approaching car horns. Haphazardly, the chief manipulated the car into the flow of traffic on the main avenue. He drove like a mad man. He wasn't about to let the Peugeot out-distance him. The gunny gripped the seat hard and for the first time in quite a while, was feeling that adrenalin rush.

The Peugeot turned first up one street then another.

"Chief," Gunny said, "You had better drop back a bit, it

looks like this guy has an evasive routine created to throw off followers. He just might turn back on us."

No sooner had the words left the Gunny's mouth than the Peugeot did a U-turn about a block ahead and was coming their direction.

The chief quickly turned right and, proceeding to the next block, turned left. He continued to the next corner where he stopped the car and they waited. He had guessed correctly. Soon they saw the Peugeot pass the intersection one block to their left as it continued the same direction in which it was originally headed.

Turning left and then right again, they could soon see the little green car ahead of them. It was quite a challenge to avoid being seen by the men in the Peugeot but they were successful and eventually they ended up on the outskirts of Cannes.

The area was an overgrown farming community which was slowly becoming suburban. Lots of private cottages had been built, filling in many of the small farm fields of the past. Giant trees lined the road indicating it as one of the age-old arteries of the city. Looking up ahead, they saw the Peugeot turn right and proceed up a lane to a cottage.

The chief pulled the car over near the entrance to the lane.

"Gunny," he said. "I want you to stay here and keep an eye on things. I'm going to approach the house and see if I can find out anything. If I don't return in a half hour, come looking for me. You'd better have that piece ready, too," he said looking at the .45.

"Aye aye, Chief," the gunny said, a look of real concern showing on his face.

He watched the chief as he approached the cottage.

That guy would have made a hell of a Marine, he thought as he watched Zabrinski cleverly move from one cover to another always keeping something between himself and the house. Eventually, the chief arrived at the cottage and the gunny lost sight of him as he went around the side of the building. Soon he appeared again and positioned himself at a particular window. He remained there peeking through the window. The gunny maintained his position and would do so unless he thought the chief needed him.

Inside the cottage, Ahmad and Ramon both dove to the floor in an automatic reaction from their previous training.

The sound was deafening as the machine-gun discharged a burst toward the window. The window sill and panes exploded in a mixture of wood and glass. The acrid smell of burnt powder filled the air.

"What the hell are you shooting at!" screamed Ahmad.

"I see Navy hat at window," shouted Asam.

Grabbing his Uzi machine pistol off a nearby table, Ahmad ordered Asam to exit the back door and go around the house. He said he would approach from the other direction. Ramon followed Ahmad.

With their weapons at the ready they approached the front of the cottage. Lying under the window, they found the body of Chief Zabrinski. Blood splattered the ground and the chief's body was covered with wood and glass fragments.

Asam approached the chief and rolled his body over with his boot.

"He is dead," he remarked.

"That's the master-at-arms of the Venture!" Ramon blurted out.

"He has followed us," said Ahmad, "We must leave immediately, he may not be alone! I'll get the car. Ramon, help Asam gather the training materials, quickly!" he shouted.

The gunny was leaning against the car with his back to the cottage as he heard the burst of the automatic weapon. He dropped to the ground as he drew his .45 from the holster.

Peeking over the hood of the car he saw the two armed men approaching the window where he had last seen the chief. He couldn't tell if Zabrinski was there or had escaped so he held his spot.

They suddenly started talking and two ran back in the cottage and one went for the car. As the car pulled up to the door, the sun reflecting off the windshield illuminated the shady front of the cottage.

There lying in the flower bed, the gunny could see the crumpled body of Chief Zabrinski.

The other two came running out of the cottage and quickly climbed inside the car. Before the car door closed, the Peugeot was rapidly accelerating down the lane toward the gunny. He knew what he had to do.

Stepping into the path of the speeding car, he raised his Colt and was able to get off one shot before having to dive to the side. As the car sped past, the ground around him erupted in multiple explosions of flying dirt, as the AK-47 answered his challenge. With reckless abandon, the Peugeot careened onto the road and rapidly accelerated away.

Jumping up, the gunny ran to the road and, taking his time, fired seven more times at the fleeing car. The back window of the car was blown completely out but the car continued on down the road.

When the back window of the Peugeot exploded, Ramon spun around from his front seat position to see Asam kneeling on the back seat, blocking the window with his body. He watched as bullet after bullet struck him.

Turning to Ramon, Asam shouted, "Remember Ramon. . . you must . . . for Islam!"

At that instant, his head exploded as another bullet struck him. His huge body slumped forward onto the back seat. He had gladly given his life to protect Ramon, to assure his success.

"I will, Asam, " he said under his breath. "I swear on the name of Allah!"

23

It couldn't have been a more wonderful day for Matt and Lee. Matt wasn't kidding when he said he knew the area well, she thought.

After checking into their hotel, he had driven her down through the old part of Nice and around the waterfront of the old port. Next, they visited the castle of Monaco and in the afternoon they had stopped by the newer part of the Principality, Monte Carlo.

She had wanted to spend some time in the gambling casino but it was too early and even if it hadn't been, they didn't have the proper attire.

This is an amazing place, she thought, All the majestic palaces, the fantastic villas, luxurious shops, and the flowered terraces ablaze with color and lined with swaying palm trees. It's hard for me to imagine, she thought, that the residents of

Monaco pay no taxes and are not required to do any military service. This tiny little state only takes up three hundred and seventy-five acres. Ah, yes, the land of the rich and famous.

Matt had pointed out Prince Ranier's motor yacht while they were overviewing the harbor.

"That's the Prince's yacht, it's the largest in the harbor. "It's the law here," he said. "Other yachts are welcome as long as they are smaller."

"Really?" she said, then she realized he was kidding and she poked him in the ribs for making her feel gullible.

She liked Matt. Actually *liked* wasn't a strong enough word. She was attracted to him the very first time they had met, near the beach. She felt really good when he was around. He had a way of doing things the way she did and it gave her the feeling of having known him for a long time.

She was sitting on the bed with a towel around her head and another wrapped around her body. Matt was in the shower washing off the day's hot sun and misty salt spray that coated everything here along the coast. He had given her first chance at the shower and that gave her the opportunity to dress while he was taking his turn.

She had something else on her mind. They had laughed and talked all day as lovers might do but he hadn't touched her once. He was treating her as if she were the fair maiden and he the charming knight. She was about to change all that. Walking through the bathroom door, he saw her sitting there.

"Oh, I'm sorry, I thought you would be dressed by now. I'll just wait in here until you finish."

"I am finished," she said.

Getting up from the bed, she approached Matt unwrapping the towel from her head. Her auburn hair cascaded over her shoulders. She stepped directly in front of him putting her arms around his neck, and pressing her lips and body against him.

Matt had hoped she felt the same way he was feeling, but he was determined to let her make the first move. He didn't want to spoil the harmony of their being together by being too forward with her. Everything had been too perfect to spoil.

Leading him over to the bed she turned to him and said, "We won't be needing this for a while."

Reaching up between her breasts, she released the towel. As it fell to the floor Matt almost gasped out loud as he was taken in by her beauty. In his eyes, her figure was approaching perfection. He could immediately feel the charge of electricity as it passed through him, ending in his groin.

He took her in his arms and kissed her long and deep. She was supple, responding to him and as his lips trailed from her mouth to her ear she began a soft moan. He continued the journey with his lips, down her neck toward her breasts. He could feel her becoming unsteady, her knees weakening.

Stepping back, she reached for his towel.

"We won't need this either," she said.

With a flick of her fingers the towel dropped to the floor.

Looking down at him she smiled and said, "But we will need that."

They made love all night, sharing their bodies and spirits. First giving, then taking, they feasted on one another until dawn.

They had breakfast in bed the next morning and the rest of the day was spent in each other's arms. Talking, laughing, touching, and sharing that time and place together.

They were at the check-out desk at seven the following morning, having decided to get an early start back to Cannes.

Lee felt obligated to return and help Frank close down the operation. There were maps and books to be packed and she had to notify the landlord of the building. They decided to delay breakfast until they were down the road a little way.

Lee snuggled next to Matt, enjoying his nearness. Reaching up with her lips she put her tongue in his ear and said coyly, "I'm starving, Matt, but I'll settle for breakfast."

He laughed as a tingle shot down his spine.

"I'd better pull over while I can and feed the hungry tigress."

Passing through the small town of Antibes, about midway to Cannes, they spotted a cafe. The parking lot was filled so he was forced to park near the highway.

Matt put the car in park, pulled on the emergency brake and reached for the ignition key. It happened so fast that neither Matt or Lee could do anything but watch. There was a tremendous explosion as the hood of the car blew completely off the Mercedes. The ensuing fire was an inferno. With the key still in the on position, the electric fuel pump continued to feed the flames and within a matter of seconds the entire front of the car was consumed.

In shock, Matt and Lee immediately scrambled directly out the back of the convertible. The heat was so great that it singed their hair and clothes.

People came running out of the cafe pointing and talking. One of them ran back inside to call for help.

"Are you all right?" someone asked as they approached the building.

"Yeah, I think so," Matt gasped. Turning, he looked at Lee. "Are you okay?"

"Well, I might have to wear a wig and false eyelashes for a while but other than that, everything appears to be here."

The fire truck arrived about twenty minutes later. The car was nothing but a big pile of smoldering junk. The firemen pulled out a hose and cautiously sprayed down the debris.

The two of them were soon being grilled with questions. The investigating police officer seemed suspicious about how quickly and violently the fire had occurred. He asked if anyone would want to harm them. Looking at one another, they assured him there wasn't.

He was kind enough to give them a ride to the car rental agency. They acquired another car and three hours later were once again on the road to Cannes.

"I'm worried," Lee said, "that's twice in two days that we have almost been killed. It could explain why the Peugeot cut us off the other day. Just think, we probably would never have gotten out of that car if we had been on this narrow highway at cruise speed."

"And thank God for convertibles," Matt added.

Matt was worried too. His foot pressed down harder on the accelerator. A knot formed in his stomach as they returned to Lee's apartment.

Pulling up in front of the apartment they both hurried up the walk toward the doorman.

"Good day, Miss James," he said, tipping his hat.

"Has anything unusual occurred here since we left?" she asked.

"Nothing out of the ordinary. This is about as peaceful a place as you could find to live," he replied.

"Good, thank you," she said.

Hurrying to the elevator she punched the call button multiple times as if it would make the car move faster. An eternity later, the door finally opened. Stepping aboard, she pressed number three, several times. She glanced nervously at Matt.

The door of the apartment stood slightly open. They entered cautiously, flicking on the light.

The place was a wreck.

In the living room, bookcases lay tipped over. Ugly slashes ripped the sofa and chairs. All their official papers had vanished. The maps and blue prints of the Venture were gone.

Making a sweep of the apartment, they found more of the

same. Someone had taken great pleasure in wrecking the place. When they came to the kitchen, they discovered a grisly sight. There was blood all over the floor, cabinets, and along the baseboards.

"Oh, no!" Lee cried out. "Poor Frank, they must have taken him. From the amount of blood, it's doubtful he is still alive."

"There's no question in my mind now that our little accidents were not accidents at all," Matt said.

"We've got to notify Tom as soon as possible," she responded.

Lee found the phone under a pile of broken furniture and was about to call when she suddenly stopped in her tracks, staring at the door.

A man stood there, or what was left of one. His clothes were torn and wrinkled, he had blood on his face and hands. Underneath the blood and dirt of his battered face, a big smile suddenly appeared.

"Frank!" Lee cried. "You're alive!" She bounded across the room to hug him.

"Easy," he said, not letting Lee hug him too hard. "My ribs are a bit sore."

He moved slowly to a chair that Matt righted for him and sat down. His face was really battered and one eye completely swollen shut.

"I had some visitors earlier today," he told them. "I had completed packing all the security materials and had taken them to the airport for shipment back to Washington. As I came down the hall to the apartment here, I heard voices inside. Not thinking, I assumed it was you two so I barged right in to find these two guys throwing things around. Before I knew what was happening, I had the barrel of an Uzi stuck in my face. One held the gun on me while this big guy — the other one called him Abu — kept working me over. He seemed to take great pleasure in it. He kept saying, 'This is for

Hassam, and this is for Hassam,' each time he hit me. I must have lost consciousness for a while." His non-swollen eye closed for a moment.

"Suddenly I felt cold water splashing on me. They had dragged me into the kitchen and were dumping water on me. Through the fog of regaining consciousness I heard Abu say, 'You stay awake, dirty infidel, I kill you nice and slow like my brother die when you shoot him in the stomach.' I realized my butt was grass if I didn't do something fast."

"What happened next?" Lee asked breathlessly.

"I figured he wanted to beat me to death and as long as I was unconscious, he would continue to revive me. I pretended to pass out again. His friend wasn't paying very close attention and had begun to look around in the cabinets, probably for something to eat.

"They obviously hadn't searched me at all. I reached down to my ankle and found my .38 snubnose still in its holster. I pulled it out and when Abu turned around with the water, I gave him a headache — two I think! The other asshole had set his pistol down while he ate some crackers or something and when he reached for it, I shot him too."

Lee touched his arm sympathetically.

"I called our counterparts with the French government," Frank continued, "and they were here in no time flat. They removed the bodies and took me to have a quick checkup down at the hospital, and *voila*, here I am, battered but alive.

"We will have a lot of explaining to do to the French Security Agency. They know those two were terrorists. Now they know we're involved in some kind of anti-terrorist activity. That's not the reason we gave them for our presence here. Tom will have to explain our way out of this one; that's his job."

"There were two attempts on our lives over the last two days also," Lee said to Frank.

She filled him in on what happened.

"Well, I'm glad they didn't succeed," Frank said. "They know we're onto their little scheme. If this doesn't prove to the director that we need to actively continue our investigation, I don't know what does!" He groaned as he pulled himself out of the chair.

"I hurt in places I didn't even know I had. I'm going to take a shower and clean myself up."

"Good idea, Frank," Matt said. "We'll see about straightening up this place before I have to return to the ship."

Lee looked at Matt sadly as Frank left the room. She knew it would be a long time until she saw Matt again, maybe months, maybe never.

"Okay, sailor," she said as the tears began to well up in her eyes. "Let's clean this mess up."

"Aye aye, Lieutenant," he said with a loving smile.

24

The gunny ran up the lane toward the cottage. Kneeling near the chief, he held his fingers on the chief's carotid artery.

"Man what a mess," he whispered.

There was a pulse. It was very faint but he could feel one. Zabrinski had been struck by two or three bullets in the shoulder. Another had taken a nick out of his left ear and still another had plowed a long crease, just above his left ear, across the side of his head.

Taking the chief's belt off, the gunny wadded up his handkerchief and put it under the chief's left arm. Next, he wrapped the belt around the shoulder thereby pressing the handkerchief against the pressure point for the arm. The bloodflow from the wound slowed greatly.

Removing his pistol from the holster, he pressed the thumb release, dropped the empty magazine and inserted another. Pulling the slide back, he chambered a round.

He threw open the back door of the cottage and entered with the .45 ready. He quickly searched the cottage and finding it empty, looked for the phone. After an eternity waiting for the operator, he slammed down the phone realizing he was wasting valuable time.

Returning to the chief, he picked him up in his arms and carried him down the lane to the car. After gently laying him in the back seat, he jumped in and started the motor. Placing the gearshift into drive, he floored the accelerator while making a U-turn.

Driving as fast as the car would go, he backtracked up the road that had brought them there. He wasn't at all sure of his location since they had followed the Peugeot to get there. Coming upon the edge of the city, he saw lots of activity. Almost passing a gas station, he slammed on the brakes. While sliding, he swerved into the station, almost hitting a gas pump. The customers dove for cover.

Across the street, two police officers sat in their vehicle. The officers immediately pulled across to the station to apprehend this obviously inebriated driver.

The gunny was never so happy to see the police. He showed them the chief, and after a quick explanation the police directed him to follow. With warning sirens blasting, they drove through town eventually arriving at the closest hospital. One of the officers ran inside and shortly was followed back by an emergency team with a gurney. After a quick assessment, Zabrinski was rolled directly to surgery.

The gunny sat in the waiting room for hours. The police officers took a statement from him as he explained everything he knew about the shooting. He told them the chief was shot while approaching the house and pretty much stuck to the rest of the story as it really happened. He explained that they had gone there to arrest a sailor off the Venture who was supposedly armed and dangerous, and that was the reason he accompanied the chief master-at-arms. The explanation even sounded pretty good to him and the police seemed to accept it without a hitch.

The head surgeon appeared in the waiting room after about five hours. He asked if anyone had accompanied Zabrinski.

"Right here!" the gunny said.

"Your friend had a hard time of it but he will survive. He lost a lot of blood. Your application on the pressure point most assuredly saved him. He still required all the blood we had on hand. We've been able to repair his shoulder although it will require a lot of physical therapy in the future.

"Our main concern is the bullet crease across the left side of his head. This has caused considerable swelling in the lining of the brain and this pressure will keep him unconscious until it goes down. That's about the total of it. I would suggest that you return to your ship and notify your medical people. I'm sure your doctors will want to examine him as soon as possible."

The gunny returned to the ship and, knowing the captain was aware of the chief's investigation, he went directly to the captain's in-port cabin. He reported the shooting, the location of the cottage as nearly as he could remember it, and the shots he had fired at the fleeing car. He told the captain of Chief Zabrinski's condition in the hospital.

"I will notify our chief surgeon to get over there immediately and look into the situation. We'll be pulling out of here in two days and if the chief can safely accompany us without any risk to his health, it is imperative that he be here. I must know who the man was that he was following," said the captain.

"I wish I could tell you, sir," the gunny replied. "The chief was about to point him out to me when the guy got picked up, so I never saw him."

"Well thank you, Gunny, you can return to your regular duties," the captain said.

"Aye aye, sir," the gunny responded as he snapped to attention and presented the salute.

The following morning Commander Thompson, along with another doctor and two corpsmen, went to the French hospital with the hopes of retrieving the chief. Chief Zabrinski had regained consciousness but couldn't remember a thing.

The doctors decided to leave him there one more day before moving him. They would then transfer him to the Venture where he could convalesce under the care of the aviation surgeons and the ship's neurologist.

On the following day, the chief's memory hadn't improved. It was going to require some time but the captain felt that when the chief did come around, he would be able to identify the terrorist.

25

The Venture left Cannes harbor that Tuesday morning, July 30th. All the crew had reported back aboard. There was the usual fanfare from a small group of French people who knew the ship would be returning to the U.S. Another carrier would take its place for the next six month tour. The Sixth Fleet carriers had followed this routine since the end of World War II.

Chief Zabrinski was brought aboard just before sailing. He was responding as well as could be expected. His short term memory was still affected. He couldn't remember anything that had occurred in the last six months. He was made comfortable in the sick bay and the captain assigned a Marine guard to him around the clock.

The Venture had been at sea for one day. At ten hundred hours that morning, the boatswain's whistle announced that all hands assigned to man-the-rail duties must report to their assigned stations. Time for the Turnover.

Turnover was a traditional ceremony performed any time one ship officially relieved another. In this case, another attack class carrier the U.S.S. Everiss CVA 44, was assuming the watch. The Venture crew were going home — they thought.

Ramon stood at his assigned station on the flight deck as the two carriers approached each other. The bright sun forced everyone to squint from the glare. A cool breeze blew across the flight deck helping to relieve the heat.

The entire flight deck perimeter was lined with sailors in their whites. All were standing at parade rest. Looking at the U.S.S. Everiss, Ramon could see the white outline of the crew duplicating the ceremony on that ship as well. This was considered the highest honor that one crew could bestow on another.

Ramon's thoughts drifted back to the events of the past several days. It was like a dream. Meeting Ahmad and his brother Asam. His intensive introduction to nuclear reactors. The shoot-out and the escape, with the heroic death of Asam.

He had liked Asam, with his bearlike appearance, big mustache and broken English. He might have seemed slow but how committed to the cause he was! Ramon thought of his promise to Asam at the moment he died.

"I will not fail him or Islam," he said to himself.

As the two ships came abreast of each other, the public address system called for honors.

"On deck! A-tten—tion!"

"P-r-e-s-e-n-t — Arms!"

"H-a-n-d — Salute!"

Echoed across the water they heard the same.

"On deck! A-tten—tion!"

"P-r-e-s-e-n-t — Arms!"

"H-a-n-d — Salute!"

As the two mighty carriers passed there was a silence broken only by the sound of the water churned up by each ship as the giant screws slowly drove the carriers forward. Shortly after passing, the announcement came.

"O-r-d-e-r — Arms!"

Next, the boatswain whistle sounded throughout the ship. "Secure from stations."

The neat white line around the flight deck broke into a thousand pieces as the men returned to their regular duties. Most enlisted men went down to their compartments, changing from whites to dungarees, which was almost always the uniform of the day when at sea.

The 1MC, as the shipwide announcement system was called, crackled a few times and suddenly the ship came alive with the captain's voice.

"Men," he said. "This is the Captain speaking, we've just completed our six month assignment in the Mediterranean and I wanted to take this opportunity to thank you for a job well done.

"I know it was hard work at times but because of your outstanding performance, we have set more records than any other sixth fleet carrier in history.

"Just two weeks ago, we on-replenished more stores, ammunition and fuel than has ever been moved before. We broke each of the individual records and we did all three in one day. It will be a long time, if ever, that such an achievement is again accomplished. Your performance was exemplary.

"I know that a lot of you are anxious to return home to your wives and sweethearts and a well earned rest as is normally the case . . ."

Suddenly a silence fell across the ship. Not a word was spoken as all ears turned toward the speakers.

"However," he interjected, "we are going to make a little

detour. The Venture, along with two nuclear guided missile escorts, the Dogeet and the Tracker, have been asked to perform a special favor for America.

"Some fifty-five years ago, sixteen first line battleships were sent around the world to test their capabilities and to attract international attention toward the modern technology of American seapower. This fleet sailed forty-six thousand miles in fourteen months.

"We have been asked to repeat that accomplishment. We will do it, however, in sixty-five days. It will require our working even harder than we have been, as the demand shall be great."

Groans filled Ramon's compartment.

"We shall be conducting underway air power demonstrations around Africa, through Southern Asian and Pacific waters and up the east coast of South America," the captain continued. "The cruise will be a conclusive demonstration of the special global mobility and self-sufficiency of nuclear powered surface ships. It will serve as striking evidence of the enormous power possessed by the United States.

"It will also be a great diplomatic gesture as well. The Venture will serve as a roving ambassador whose actions and abilities will speak for all the people of our country.

"We will assemble a viewing area on the 0-11 deck to seat our visitors so they may view these demonstrations from a relatively close range. These at-sea demonstrations will be repeated for local dignitaries of the various countries participating as we pass their shores. These shipboard visits will, of course, require our keeping the Venture in a state of tip top cleanliness. It will be a busy sixty-five days, as we have scheduled thirty-two demonstrations during that period."

The men looked around in dismay. No leave for sixty-five more days!

"The concentrated effort will be broken up by liberty calls

in Karachi, Pakistan; Sydney, Australia; and Rio de Janeiro, Brazil. We shall complete the circumnavigation with our arrival in New York Harbor. A grand gala is planned for our homecoming to top off the event.

"I know that a lot of you are disappointed with the delay but under the circumstances will appreciate the honor bestowed upon the Venture and its accompanying ships. I know you will do your best as you always have.

"Good luck. Let us have a safe journey. That is all."

Only one hour after being relieved of duty with the Sixth Fleet, Venture welcomed aboard her first underway visitors. They arrived to witness a demonstration of naval sea and air power.

The purpose of the record-breaking on-rep suddenly became apparent.

26

Matt was working in his water test lab when he received the call.

"Water Lab. BT1 Blackthorn speaking," Matt answered.

"BT1 Blackthorn, this is Captain Halliday. If you're not tied up with anything important at the moment, would you please report to my at-sea cabin right away."

"Yes sir," Matt responded, "I'll be right there."

Matt locked the water shed, as he called it, and climbed the three ladders that brought him to the hangar deck. Proceeding forward on the port side, he entered the ladder well that took him up to the Island where the captain would be waiting. He was pretty sure what the captain wanted to talk about. He recalled Tom telling him that the captain would be notified of his taking Mike Young's place.

The captain's Marine orderly was standing outside the cabin door.

"Please state your business," he said crisply.

"I'm BT1 Blackthorn," Matt responded, "Captain Halliday sent for me."

"Wait here please," the corporal said. He returned shortly and admitted Matt to the cabin.

Entering, he was impressed by the quality of everything. This was his first time in the cabin and he gazed enviously at the luxury.

Dark mahogany paneling covered the bulkheads. The overhead was a suspended ceiling, tiled in sound-proof panels. The deck was covered with a deep pile carpet. A large couch stood along one wall and a big deep chair along another. He could picture the captain sitting in the comfortable chair reading a good book when time permitted.

At the back of the room the captain sat behind a large cherry wood desk, the top of which was decorated by various papers and documents. Captain Halliday looked up from something he was writing and said, "Come in Blackthorn and sit down please."

Matt took a seat in the chair indicated by the captain just in front of the desk.

"Blackthorn," he began. "I was notified by Tom Barnes of the NSC that due to the death of their agent, Mike Young, they have asked you to cooperate with them in assuming his role here aboard the Venture.

"I think it highly commendable that you are in agreement with them although it made me damn mad when I learned this had transpired without my prior permission. You're not a trained agent and I feel this puts you into a dangerous situation."

"I feel confident I can handle it, sir."

"I was informed that you had been thoroughly briefed regarding explosive threats. I was also told you went through some training during your week of leave on terrorist history, activities, and other related subjects."

"Yes, sir."

"If we had the time to replace you with someone more qualified, I wouldn't allow this to continue, but Barnes feels you can do the job. I do want you to understand your chain of command. Remember that you are first an enlisted man aboard the Venture and secondly assisting the NSC people. You are to let me know of any developments before you notify them.

"Up until a week ago," he continued, "I wasn't sure that all of this amounted to anything. After recent developments, I'm convinced otherwise. A while back, I assigned the chief master-at-arms to investigate the possibility of this deep sleeper. I'm not sure what he discovered, but the other day he was shot on the outskirts of Cannes while observing some kind of activity. He is currently recovering in sick bay. His wounds were pretty serious and it will be a while before he gets back on his feet."

"Sorry to hear it, sir," Matt said.

"The problem is, one of the bullets creased his head and he has lost his most recent memory. He can't recall why he was there or even being assigned to the investigation. I want you to assist him in any way you can to help him remember. I have authorized you to visit him in sick bay as often as you need. The Marine gunny has been notified of the same.

"The doctors say he could regain his memory at any time. If he remembers who he was following or what he observed at the time of the shooting, we will surely need to take action ASAP.

"I have notified your department that I have temporarily assigned you TAD to the master-at-arms office. The reactor department will have someone take over your duties in the meantime. You are free to spend your time on this matter.

"Let me know directly of any developments. Do you have any questions?"

"No, sir," Matt replied, "I understand."

"Good," the captain said. "Thank you for coming and my compliments for your efforts, I know you didn't have to do this. Your father will be proud of you. I served under him before he retired. When this is all ironed out, he will be the first to know."

"Thank you, sir," Matt said as he saluted and excused himself.

Matt made his way down to the second deck to sick bay. He should see Chief Zabrinski right away.

As Matt entered the aisle where the chief's rack was located, he was intercepted by the Marine guard. After the guard had examined Matt's identification he passed him on through.

The chief was sitting up on his rack. His left arm and shoulder were immobilized by bandages. The left side of his face was also covered.

"Chief Zabrinski?" Matt said. "My name is Matt Blackthorn. I'm a Boiler Tender normally assigned to the Reactor Laboratory Division."

Matt sat down on an empty rack opposite the chief.

"Looks like you've been through holy hell, Chief. I sure hope you're feeling better than you look."

"There's not much pain," the chief replied. "The doctors keep me doped up pretty good. What can I do for you, Matt?"

"Chief, I've been ordered by the captain to work on the investigation that you were on when you got shot. As soon as you're feeling better and can get around, I hope we can work together to get to the bottom of this," Matt said.

"To be honest with you, Matt, I don't even remember working on any investigation. The last thing I remember was sending some prisoners down to the brig, which I understand occurred over three weeks ago. The doctors say as soon as the swelling around my brain goes down I should begin to recover my recent memory."

"I'll be stopping by every few days, Chief, to see how you're progressing. As your memory begins to return, I can do your legwork for you until you get on your feet again. Here's my phone number. If you need me for anything at all, please call."

Wishing the chief a speedy recovery, Matt made his way up to the office of the master-at-arms.

Jack Johnson, the assistant MA, was sitting at his desk. Matt introduced himself and before he could say another word, Jack said, "I've been instructed by the captain's office to cooperate with you in any way I can. So, what can I do for you, Matt?"

"I need to know what the chief was working on before he was shot," Matt said.

"The truth is, I haven't the least idea. The chief told me that when he was at liberty to discuss it he would. I can tell you this. One night a week or so ago, just before we pulled into Cannes, he called me at taps and had me meet him on the hangar deck. He had me follow him through the G-division compartment. He told me to return after taps and bring him a specific garbage can that he had pointed out. I was not to be seen taking it. I had to wait a long time till everyone was asleep but I got the can and brought it up here to the office.

"We dumped it on the floor and picked every piece of paper out of it we could find. The chief seemed to be interested in the pieces of a letter that had been torn up. After we picked those out he thanked me and told me to hit it. That's all I know."

"So you never got to see the letter later and he didn't mention what was in it?"

"Not once. I looked through the chief's desk after the accident but haven't found a damn thing." Jack said.

"Okay. Thanks, Jack, I'll be working out of this office for a while so I'll see you often. Let me know of anything you discover."

"No sweat," Johnson replied.

"Johnson, can you show me that trash can?"

They went to the compartment in question.

"Who's assigned here?" Matt asked.

"Hangar Deck Ordnance crew."

As they were leaving the compartment Johnson stopped and turned to Matt. "One thing I didn't mention."

"What's that?" Matt asked.

"There was a fatal accident in the head assigned to this compartment. A guy named Smith apparently slipped and busted his head wide open on the tile floor."

"And?"

"He slept on that bottom rack, next to the trash can."

27

The following days turned into weeks as the Venture and accompanying ships continued their historic voyage around the world.

Dignitaries first came aboard from Rabat, Morocco, then three days later, on the third of August, the representatives of Dakar, Senegal. The following day, August fourth, two air displays were presented, first to the military leaders of Freetown, Sierra Leone and later to a group from Monrovia, Liberia.

Abidjan, Ivory Coast was next, on the fifth. Finally there was a welcome ten day break in the activity. Everyone had worked long hours to prepare and clean up after each of the displays. The crew were beginning to call themselves "Halliday's Traveling Sea Circus."

Matt lent a hand in the Reactor Lab due to the heavy load.

He still continued during his free time to explore various leads that he developed.

The chief was slowly improving and was walking around the sickbay quite a bit as his strength returned. His memory was also returning very slowly. He could now remember meeting with the captain and being assigned the task of finding the terrorist.

Matt worked with him, filling in the gaps with information he knew from the NSC group. He explained his position with the NSC, and he and the chief were slowly becoming friends. Matt spent hours with the chief, playing chess and tossing ideas around that might help the chief recall something.

Matt became familiar with the hangar deck crew personnel but as yet didn't suspect any one of them in particular. He would just have to wait until the chief recalled more.

On August fifteenth, Nairobi, Kenya was the next country to be wined and dined.

The show had evolved into quite a display. It began with the brief stopping of the ship. The audience gathered on the fantail. A smoke flare would be tossed off and the order — full ahead — given.

The Venture came alive like a mammoth sleeping giant awakening after its winter hibernation. A vibration slowly traveled from one end of the ship to the other beginning at the fantail. As the four giant five-bladed screws began their rotation, the ship almost jumped up and down at the aft end. It slowly began to move, and in only minutes the smoke flare would become a tiny trail in the distance.

The audience was next escorted to their viewing platform on the 0-11 level. With everyone seated and comfortable, the airpower demonstration began.

Several jets flew by, dropping smoke flares ahead and to the side of the Venture. Aircraft from the different squadrons made various weapons runs on the targets.

Some demonstrated low level drops with fire bombs. Others approached from higher altitudes and in sharp dives fired salvos of rockets and 20mm cannons.

One bombing demonstration was called lofting. This type of bombing was used to throw a bomb in a high arc similar to the effect of a mortar shell. It was a good display of the pilot's flying skills.

The aircraft approached the target at low level, making it difficult to track the aircraft on radar. At a specified distance from the target, the jet made a sudden vertical ascension. Several hundred feet later, the bomb released automatically while the aircraft still pointed upward. The bomb could be seen leaving the jet and continuing its flight as a result of the launching speed of the aircraft and inertia. It would fly a long high arc and hopefully fall on the target. By then, the jet would have turned back and be well clear of the effect.

This technique was used for launching the medium class hydrogen bombs that were housed in the belly of this whale — something the U.S. Navy would neither confirm nor deny.

Next came a demonstration of the sidewinder missiles. Several reconnaissance jets crossed the bow several hundred feet above the ship. At a good distance from the ship, they ejected high candle parachute flares. The small parachutes blossomed open and, as they slowly drifted toward the water, the brightly burning flares could easily be seen from the observation deck.

Shortly thereafter, several more jets crossed the bow and fired sidewinder missiles at the parachute flares. The sidewinder, being attracted by the heat from the flare, would fly a coil pattern toward the flare and, almost without fail, the flare would disappear in a violent explosion.

The show finale was a low level fly-by of various aircraft in very tight formation. This closely followed by three jets equipped with colored smoke, each leaving a trail of red, white and blue. All very patriotic and one hundred percent American.

Karachi, West Pakistan, was to be the first port call. The Venture would be arriving there on August 20th. The ship would anchor out in the bay there and a liberty call would take place to give the crew a few days of R & R.

Three days before Karachi, the mail plane arrived bringing the first mail since the cruise began in the Mediterranean.

There was a letter for Ramon from his mom.

Dear Ramon,
How are things, my son? God has always protected you from harm as I'm sure he will continue to do. Now devotion is even more important as the world seems in a turmoil. Giving always returns two fold — remember. Do endeavor now to be at your best as the long days at sea are, I'm sure, very lonely and difficult.

Enough about that — I don't wish to depress you. It will all be over soon. I think of you often and miss you dearly.
Love
Your Mom

It actually read: Hat at Ghandi Garden. It was time for lesson number two.

28

Three ships of the Pakistan Navy assigned to act as escorts greeted the Venture as it approached Karachi. They escorted the carrier into the harbor at Karachi, where difficult boating conditions limited the number of men able to get ashore for liberty to about seventeen hundred. After damaging two of the liberty launches against the accommodation ladder, it was decided to limit the liberty to those that had already arrived at the landing. Ramon was one of the lucky seventeen hundred.

This being their first port since leaving the Mediterranean, many of the crew were anxious to take in the local atmosphere. Karachi, located on the Arabian Sea, is the largest city in Pakistan and its major sea port.

They saw evidence everywhere of the hardships the country had experienced from the deluge of Muslim refugees from all parts of India after the Partition in 1947. More recently, over 2.8 million Afghan refugees burdened Pakistan's economy. Many of those settled here in Karachi. Over five million people occupied the city.

Several dozen motor-driven rickshaws parked near the landing, each covered in intricately painted flowers and ornate designs. These three wheel vehicles were the common taxi of this poor nation.

Ramon was approached by several motor rickshaw drivers all jabbering as fast as they could to get his business. After he selected one, the others dashed away to make their sales pitch to the next sailor they could stop.

"Do you know a place called Ghandi Garden?" Ramon inquired of the driver.

"Yes, to be sure," came the reply. "Please sit." He indicated that Ramon should climb aboard.

With that, the driver gave a mighty push and as the rickshaw gained speed he jumped onto the seat and popped the clutch. Making several backfire sounds, the motor started and they roared off through the crowd. He drove like a madman, constantly tooting his horn and making people jump out of the way. He seemed to enjoy it. With each near miss, he would look back at Ramon and smile, as if to gain approval and admiration from the U.S. Navy.

Ramon attempted to enjoy the scenery as they made their dash for glory. They passed the busy open-air market places and bazaars with their air of activity.

The streets were congested by many motor rickshaws like the one Ramon rode in. There were also quite a number of horse drawn carts and camels. Just about anything that would roll could be seen being pulled or pushed by anything with four legs. They even passed several elephants burdened with heavy loads.

Everywhere he looked there were small shops with articles of brass, carved wood pieces, inlaid items and silk fabrics.

There was considerable street entertainment in the form of dancing monkeys and snake charmers. It was a different world here, slower, brilliantly colored, and very, very old in tradition. It was like stepping back in time.

To Ramon, it was the closest resemblance to his home land that he had visited thus far. He felt a strange stirring inside. A feeling of belonging and yet not belonging.

Mostly men occupied the streets. What women he saw were covered in black, their faces hidden as their Islamic religion dictated. Here he could see the proper respect paid to Mohammed.

They finally arrived at Ghandi Garden and Ramon was surprised to see large beautiful gardens. He had thought it might be a restaurant or something like that. He paid the driver and started to enter the garden when he felt someone tap him on the shoulder. As he turned, he heard a familiar voice.

"Mr. Hat at your service, Ramon," Ahmad said with a smile.

Ramon followed Ahmad a short distance to a waiting car. Not far from the Ghandi Garden, Ahmad turned onto a side street and almost immediately turned again, driving through metal gates that quickly closed behind them. A large concrete building stood before them.

"This is our training center here in Karachi, Ramon. Welcome," he said.

Inside, several members of Ahmad's group greeted Ramon. They all stared at his uniform, mesmerized.

"Before you decide to shoot holes in this," Ramon said, "let me take it off."

That broke the silence as they all laughed.

Ahmad was prepared for Ramon. A slide projector and screen waited. Ramon sat on a pile of cushions on the floor and accepted tea from one of the men.

"We have little time," Ahmad said, "so let's begin. "Ramon, did you know that Pakistan has its own nuclear reactor? It supplies the majority of the power used in this country. We, of course, have friends that work with the reactor and this has been our source of knowledge which I, at our previous meeting, gave to you.

"Pakistan has been denied nuclear technology by other nations because it refuses to sign the Nuclear Nonproliferation Treaty and doesn't allow international monitoring of its nuclear facilities. Nevertheless it proceeds, perhaps slowly, but very surely. Tell me Ramon, have you been able to approach the ship's reactor areas? What do you think your chances of success would be to tamper with one without being discovered?"

"I have casually walked as close as I can to those areas," Ramon said. "But they are heavily guarded and without business in the area, I could easily be detected. The only way, I feel, would be an armed suicide assault and even then I might not reach one of them."

"Well," Ahmad said, "you know what to do should you get the opportunity. We have to discuss another matter now."

He turned on the projector and Ramon recognized a slide of the Navy's top secret Mark 67 hydrogen bomb.

"Thanks to information sold to the Russians by the two American Navy personnel we have complete schematics of this weapon. From reviewing your background training I see that you attended the nuclear weapons loading school. Did you learn anything at that school about the inner workings of this weapon?"

"No," Ramon said, "They only showed us how to load it onto the bomb rack of the transporting aircraft."

"Well basically, the hydrogen bomb is about a thousand times as powerful as the atomic bomb. You probably don't know it, Ramon, but the Mark 67 is not just a hydrogen bomb but a neutron bomb."

"I've heard this mentioned but without a need to know, I haven't been able to learn the difference. Can you explain it?" Ramon said.

"Yes," continued Ahmad. "A neutron bomb is a special type of small hydrogen bomb considered useful for battlefield or tactical conditions. It's referred to as an *enhanced radiation weapon* because the number of neutrons emitted is greater in proportion to the explosive force than in a conventional atomic or hydrogen bomb. By modification of the bomb design, the number of neutrons, which is the nuclear radiation component, along with alpha, beta, and gamma radiation can be increased.

"Neutrons are uncharged particles and will travel great distances through matter until stopped or slowed, most likely by collision with light atoms.

"Humans are susceptible to injury from neutron irradiation because the body's water molecules contain the lightest atom, hydrogen. Structures do not suffer biological changes and therefore are less prone to alteration from encounters with neutrons. A weapon that produces neutrons having a lethal or incapacitating range greater than the range of its thermal and pressure effects will be more damaging to living things than to structures."

Ramon looked confused. "Explain that."

"If, let's say, this weapon were to be detonated at the correct distance from a target, no damage at all would occur to the structures but all life within range would be altered.

"It was developed originally as a warhead on a short-range Lance missile or in an artillery shell, for use against tanks. It came into prominence in the mid-seventies when the NATO countries were faced with the prospect of overwhelming Soviet superiority on the ground, in the event of an invasion of

Western Europe. The U.S. leaders ordered full assembly and stockpiling of the weapons in 1981.

"We estimate that the Venture must carry eight or ten of these weapons. They, as you well know, are kept in the nuclear weapons spaces."

He pushed the projector control button and a cut-away drawing of the Venture appeared. It indicated the nuclear weapons spaces beginning just forward of the aft mess deck and extending down several decks.

"I know where the weapons are stored," said Ramon. "This area is under twenty-four hour Marine guard and access is limited to those with a Top Secret clearance. As you can see from the slide, there is only one way in and one way out. It would be next to impossible to get past the guard without him setting off the alarm system."

"Yes, we know that but suppose you could enter the spaces without their knowledge," Ahmad added as he scratched his hook-like nose.

"Look here," he pointed, "there is an elevator shaft that is used by the weapons department. You have access to these elevators. The elevator trunk is accessible from the mess deck. With the proper cutting torch, you could cut through the elevator well, into the magazine trunk and finally through into the nuclear weapons space. It would mean cutting through three bulkheads of quarter-inch steel. You could do it easily. If the cutting is done when activity is low in the area, two of the three walls can be done in advance, leaving the final for the time of entry."

"How could I detonate the weapon?" Ramon asked.

"Ah! that comes next in your lesson," Ahmad said confidently.

"Do you recall what a firing train is, Ramon?"

"Yes," he said. "In a Navy weapon, to make it carrier safe for an arrested landing, all weapons must have a misaligned firing train. Most weapons consist of a fuse which contains a small amount of very sensitive explosive like lead azide or fulminate of mercury.

"This, when activated, will explode setting off the booster, the next charge in the train, which is a little more stable and this in turn sets off the main charge. The booster is not moved in line with the other two until mechanically moved by either the fuse vane rotation or electrically by the pilot."

"Exactly," said Ahmad. "You remember your training well. The Mark 67 has an even more complex firing train because of its obvious potential.

"The fusing device is barometrically controlled and an accelerometer must activate it. If you don't recall from ordnance school, an accelerometer is a switch that functions after being influenced by G forces. Before the accelerometer will function, however, it must be electrically activated by the pilot with the Master Arming switch.

"Here is the way it works. Once the jet is airborne with the Mark 67 and near the target, the pilot electrically arms the weapon. This activates the accelerometer and now it can be influenced by G forces.

"The weapon is delivered via the lofting method. When the pilot is ready to launch the weapon, he arms it with a switch in the cockpit. This electrically rotates the accelerometer, aligning it in the firing train. Next he initiates a vertical climb. When the preset G force is reached, the pilot releases the weapon.

"Shortly thereafter, the accelerometer allows activation of the barometric sensitive fuse. As the weapon is tossed upward by the inertia of the launching aircraft, the fuse calibrates at that higher elevation. Beginning its descent, the fuse detects the change in pressure and at the preset pressure or altitude, the weapon detonates.

"With this system," Ahmad added, "in the event the strike

is recalled or for transporting purposes the weapon can be safely handled."

The remainder of Ramon's liberty period was spent familiarizing him with the inner workings of the Mark 67. The slides were a complete set of instructor slides used at the Mark 67 training center.

They left nothing uncovered. By the time Ramon left that afternoon, he knew as much about the Mark 67 and its fail-safe systems as the nuclear weapons technicians did.

Ahmad dropped Ramon off about a block from the landing. He told him to go to the Rio de Janeiro Yacht Club when he arrived in Rio. He would receive his final orders there.

Walking the final block along the piers was an experience in itself. The conditions were so crowded that people simply lay down next to each other on the ground to sleep. The smell was overwhelming. Laying amongst the sleeping were many dead and diseased people.

The water in the bay had become so rough that an old minesweeper, given to the Pakistan Navy by the U.S. after World War II, was being used to transport the men to the Venture. It was an extremely slow process. It carried about two hundred men each trip. Arriving at the Venture, it pulled up just close enough for the bow of the sweeper to be within jumping distance of what remained of the crushed accommodation ladder. Each time a swell brought the sweeper's bow near the ladder, two or more men jumped if time allowed. Then the bow would suddenly plunge downward some ten or twelve feet. As the bow heaved its way back upward, the next two sailors in line moved into position. It was an extremely dangerous operation but it must have been everyone's lucky day. As daylight broke across the bay all the Venture's crew were aboard and without a single injury.

The Venture was underway two hours later. Ramon

watched as Pakistan faded in their wake. Turning away, he started for the compartment. He had a lot of planning to do.

29

Six days later the Venture and her accompanying ships crossed the equator for the third time. They were headed toward a rendezvous with the British Royal Navy carrier HMS Victorious. British Naval guests toured the Venture and witnessed a short air show.

"Thank God, you're on our side!" was the comment by one of their officers.

On the 31st of August, the coast of Australia came into view, the only continent in the world occupied by a single nation.

The first visitors to arrive from the continent were from the cities of Perth and Freemantle. The Minister of the Australian Navy, as well as the Lords Mayor of Freemantle and Perth were welcomed aboard.

The guests, representing government and military, as well as extensive press coverage from other Australian cities, saw the air power show which the Venture had been staging halfway around the world.

Matt continued his visits to sickbay in the hopes of helping Chief Zabrinski with his memory. He and the chief had given up on chess and were now hot checkers competitors. They had become close friends and Matt had told him all about his romance with Lee.

Matt had received a letter from Lee. She was going to meet him in Sydney for a holiday. He couldn't wait to see her. It had now been a month since he held her in his arms and he found her occupying much of his thoughts. He was sure he loved her and when he saw her in Sydney, he planned to tell her so.

The ship was to visit Sydney for four days. This would give every man aboard the opportunity for liberty.

The chief was improving as well as expected after only one month. His shoulder was much improved but the cast made it difficult to move around. The three bullets had shattered his shoulder and he had several pins holding bones together.

Matt brought his mail each day and kept him informed about the activity going on in the master-at-arms office. Zabrinski's mind was clear as a bell and he acted perfectly normal, except for the missing two weeks prior to leaving Cannes.

"Last night I had a strange dream," he said to Matt.

"Oh?" Matt replied, "What about?"

"I was in a coffee house like the ones in the sixties. You probably wouldn't remember, or maybe you would. Anyway, this guy came in the front door leading a camel. On the camel's head was the strangest hat I've ever seen. I can't describe it for some reason but it was really weird. He walks up to me and I notice he has a dogging wrench stuck in his belt. He looks at me and says, 'I just ate rue!'" The chief looked puzzled.

"What?" Matt replied. "That doesn't make a damn bit of sense, Chief."

"You're telling me!" Zabrinski said.

"I just ate rue," Matt repeated. "It has got to mean something. What we need is one of those books on how to interpret dreams."

To Matt this was a good sign. The doctor had told him that this might happen. Scattered memories coming together, perhaps in the wrong time frame or not associated. The important thing was that they were beginning to surface at all.

Melbourne on September third, was the final underway demonstration of the cruise before reaching port at Sydney.

A Melbourne newsman presented the ship with an authentic Australian boomerang, to which Rear Admiral Strict replied, "This is just what we needed for the finishing touch to our fantastic array of armament."

Although a light rain fell and a cold wind blasted the observation area, the visitors, bundled into foul weather gear, watched the spectacle of fire power enthusiastically.

"An awe-inspiring example of the strength of the U.S. in the free world," one of them commented.

The following day, the Venture entered Sydney Harbor. At least two hundred small boats followed the giant supercarrier to her anchorage in the harbor. An estimated one hundred thousand persons jammed the fleet landing and the cliffs overlooking the harbor.

And there was always the anchor pool to look forward to. As the anchor dropped, another crewman aboard became five or six thousand dollars richer.

Prior to arrival and with the cooperation of the Royal Australian Navy, the Venture had staged an aerial fire-power demonstration off the coast of Sydney. A group of twenty-two dignitaries were flown aboard the Venture for the show. They exclaimed later that the demonstration was "first rate."

Matt couldn't wait for liberty call. He had his blond locks trimmed the night before at the ship's barber. Normally, he had his own barber, another crewman, as did many of the guys that were particular about the results. His barber had a line of about thirty guys waiting though, and Matt wasn't about to be turned back at the accommodation ladder for lack of a hair cut, so it was "take your chance time." It was a nice trim. He was surprised at the result and pleased Lee wouldn't see him looking like a skin head.

His uniform was spotless and, although he liked to roll the edge of his hat, he promised himself he wouldn't touch it until well clear of the ship since that was also a no-no.

He was privileged to leave the ship after the chiefs as he was only one step down from a chief himself. The launch ride was the longest he had ever made. He knew it was all in his head but he felt like he was having trouble breathing and his heart rate surely had to be over two hundred.

The crowded fleet landing made it impossible to see her. After turning every brunette around that wasn't already facing him, he started up the road towards town.

It was the best reception that the crew had ever received, bar none! Whole families came for the occasion. Matt was stopped several times as he walked along, by people inviting him to their homes for dinner or barbecue. It was a very rewarding feeling to be wanted somewhere.

A taxi pulled up beside him and the driver said, "Can we give you a ride, bloke?"

"No, thanks," Matt replied.

"Are you sure about that, sailor?" came Lee's voice from the back seat.

He was in the taxi before the driver could get it stopped. Into the taxi and into her arms. The driver just sat there with a smile on his face as the two lovers greeted each other.

"No hurry, you two," he said laughing. "We'll just sit here a minute until you come up for air."

Embarrassed, they both laughed and Lee gave him directions for the hotel. They wouldn't be going anywhere until they were properly reacquainted.

30

Ramon arrived at fleet landing about an hour after liberty call. He couldn't believe how many people had gathered to greet the ship. It was so crowded, he had trouble just leaving the landing.

It felt good to just walk around on dry land. He had lunch at a cafe near the landing. When he got ready to pay, the waitress smiled and said his check was compliments of the house.

He'd heard that during the second World War the American Navy had stopped the Japanese from invading Australia. These people obviously were not going to forget that, no matter how many years passed.

While walking down the street, just window shopping, he stopped to look in the window of a sporting goods store. On display, was the latest brightly colored diving gear. They carried masks, fins, snorkels and tanks. That's when the idea hit him.

Continuing up the street, he came to a clothing store. He purchased some local clothes and at the restroom of a nearby bar, he changed into them. Returning to the diving shop, he purchased a double set of scuba tanks, the necessary tools to disassemble them and a diving gear bag.

Next, he rented a car and returned to pick up the tanks. Stopping at a roadside phone booth, he looked through the business pages and found what he was looking for.

Sydney Welding Supply . . . 243 Queens Court. . . 767-2311

Tearing out the map in the back of the book, he drove across the Harbor Bridge toward North Sydney. He pulled over at a park and took the two tanks apart. Across the street from the park he noticed a hardware store. He crossed the street and spotted the paint department right away. He bought three cans of quick drying paint, white, red and green. He returned to the car, took the two bottles and, finding an inconspicuous spot, painted one red and the other green.

Two hours later, he arrived at the welding supply and an hour after that, he was on his way back toward fleet-landing with his red scuba bottle filled with acetylene, and the green one with oxygen. He had also acquired all the necessary equipment to assemble his makeshift cutting torch.

He stopped at the same park and, returning to the spot he previously used, carefully painted both bottles white once again. He lay back on the grass while waiting for the paint to dry and complimented himself on his ingenious idea. When the tanks were finally dry, he reassembled them into the scuba configuration.

Returning to fleet-landing, he persuaded a shore patrol to keep an eye on his diving gear while he returned the rented car.

Since diving gear was allowed, no questions were asked as he acted like a returning diver.

"How was the diving?" the shore patrol officer asked.

"Great," he replied. "Australia has some of the best water in the world!"

He didn't elaborate, not wanting the conversation to continue.

The boat coxswains frowned on carrying too much equipment to and from the ship because of the space it took up in the launches. Most of the divers had to wait to go ashore until the flow of the liberty hounds slowed down. Returning to the ship early was preferred before the boats began to fill up. Ramon had perfect timing. The boat was about half full and no one said a word.

Arriving back at the ship, he was lugging the tanks back up the accommodation ladder when a voice stopped him in his tracks.

"Hey, sailor, you with the scuba."

"Great, just all I need," he said under his breath, someone to notice the damp paint or ask to see inside the gear bag. Looking over his shoulder, he could see an officer approaching him with the all too familiar Shore Patrol armband.

It was a returning shore patrol officer. Ramon almost panicked. For a split second, he entertained the idea of dropping everything and running. Running where? he thought.

"Yes, sir," he responded, feeling like a kid caught with his hand in the cookie jar.

"Hold on there, let me give you a hand."

"Sure, thanks a lot, sir," Ramon replied.

With a sigh of relief, he handed the officer the gear bag and continued up the ladder.

The Officer of the Deck thinking Ramon was helping another officer to carry his scuba gear, waved him on through. Once in the hangar bay, he thanked the officer for the help and, taking the gear bag, headed for the ordnance crew coffee mess. He knew it would be empty. Everyone was either on liberty, standing watch, or in their racks.

Most everyone on the ship had a cruise chest. It was usually an empty ammo box or wooden crate where they could lock up their personal gear, like scuba for example. His cruise chest was once used for shipping 2.75 inch folding fin aircraft rockets. It was made of oak and one of the more prized choices when available. His was mostly empty and the small tanks and gear bag fit perfectly. He could move the whole box later, when he was ready for it.

31

Venture left Sydney four days later. This time, not all the crew were aboard. Eleven sailors loved Sydney and the way they were treated a bit too much. It was the largest over-the-hill-gang in the history of the Venture since its commission.

It was an embarrassment for Captain Halliday and one didn't embarrass the captain of the largest warship afloat.

Matt had used his NSC influence and remained on shore the whole four days. He and Lee couldn't have spent the time better. They didn't leave the hotel until the second day.

The days were filled with sight seeing and the evenings filled with romance. They danced under the stars, ate the local foods and had a wonderful time.

As Matt had promised himself, that first night he told Lee how he felt.

"Lee," he said, as they lay locked in each other's arms. "I hope this doesn't come out wrong but I want you to know how very much I have grown to love you. I think about you a thousand times a day. I find myself wondering what you're doing every moment and wishing we could be together all the time. I feel content when I'm with you and miserable when I'm not. I would like to think that we will have a long future together."

"Oh Matt," she responded, "you have made me so happy and I do love you too."

Nothing could have distracted the two over the next few days. They were totally mesmerized with each other.

But that final day came and they had to say goodbye for a while.

Tom had actually sent her there to get any updated information that Matt might have gathered, but he also had become aware of their feelings for each other and was playing the cupid role a little.

Lee informed Matt that she was instructed to continue on to Rio and would see Matt there when the Venture made port. It made their parting much easier. They would see each other again in about three weeks.

On the 8th of September, just one day after leaving Sydney, the Prime Minister of New Zealand and his party were brought aboard for the air demonstration.

Another nine days later the ships of the nuclear task force were rounding the infamous Cape Horn, scourge of ancient sailing ships. The Horn, famous in sailing history, was a great test of a sailor's courage, skill and endurance because of the great storms that have raged for centuries off its coast.

The Cape could be seen quite clearly, rising nearly fourteen hundred feet out of the sea, a giant rock whose upper slopes were snow covered. Sailing ships of the past had fought the vicious weather and seas for as much as five days before the Cape allowed them to pass from one ocean to the other. Many ships sank in these waters. The Venture took just one day to arrive in the South Atlantic.

On the 21st of September, the Venture entertained guests from Buenos Aires, Argentina, and later the same afternoon, another display was presented to the representatives of Montevideo, Uruguay.

The crew worked gruelling hours to meet the great demand for the airshows. Especially the weapons department. The assembly and movement of all the rockets, fire bombs, smoke bombs, low drag bombs, 20mm cannon ammunition and accompanying equipment kept the men working around the clock on many days.

The various components had to be taken out of their respective storage areas, assembled, loaded on bomb carts and wheeled to areas where they were made easily accessible. No one, including Ramon, seemed to have time for anything but working, sleeping and eating.

Ramon had formulated his plan to access the nuclear weapons spaces. After he cut through the three bulkheads, he would open the access plates on one of the weapons and remove the accelerometer. His intention was to then adjust the barometric fuse to zero and by using their own test gear, he would detonate the weapon.

The sudden realization that he might die soon was a new feeling for him. He began to view each day differently. The taste of the food was somehow different. When he looked around, he saw more colors. Sounds seemed different somehow. It was probably a reaction that all people experienced who realized that death was eminent. He felt that to give his life for what he believed was the greatest sacrifice that a human could offer.

They will all be sacrificing their lives soon for what they

believe, he thought. It's a shame they can't experience this sense of wonder I'm feeling.

32

The 23rd of September, just two more days at sea brought the task force to the final port call before the States. Thousands of Brazilians covered the famous beaches of Rio de Janeiro to witness the arrival of the Venture and its accompanying ships.

The ships anchored in Guanabara Bay for a two day port visit. Venture fired a twenty-one gun salute to the city and shortly thereafter a Brazilian flying team circled over the three ships in a series of precision maneuvers. Man-the-rail was called as a special greeting to the city.

Lee waited for Matt at fleet landing. They embraced as if they hadn't seen each other in years.

"Come on," she said. "I've rented a car and I've found the nicest bungalow near the beach."

As they walked toward the car with their arms around

each other, they both noticed the envy in the eyes of many of the sailors going on liberty.

Other eyes also watched the two. Ahmad and one of his men followed a short distance behind. He had failed in his earlier attempt and they couldn't afford to have these people interfere now that Ramon was about to make his final move.

As Lee and Matt pulled away from the curb in the rental car, Ahmad and his man followed a half block behind.

Ahmad followed them to a small cottage several miles away. He and his man watched from a distance as the lovers got out of the car and went inside. It was in a secluded area and would be the perfect place for what he had in mind. That would come later, right now he had to get to the Rio Yacht Club to meet Ramon.

Ramon was sitting at a table on the veranda outside the cafe of the Yacht Club. It was a beautiful place and almost took his mind away from his heavy burden for the moment. He could see Christ of the Andes, a giant statue, on the mountain in the distance. Thirty or forty brightly colored boats lined the floating piers in front of him. The breeze ever so gently moved the leaves of the coconut palms that lined the water front.

"I could take a lot of this," he said under his breath.

Ahmad entered his view suddenly. He didn't say anything, just nodded his head in the direction of the parking lot and walked off.

Ramon waited a couple of minutes and followed. They drove quite a distance across the city to an area that was inhabited by Arab immigrants.

"We are safe here," Ahmad said, leading Ramon into a small white house on a narrow side street.

They spent most of the morning reviewing the weak points of the reactor and the Mark 67. Ahmad was convinced, from Ramon's answers, that he was prepared.

"Ramon, I know that you're ready and will do the best you can. The committee has selected the location."

Ramon felt his excitement building.

"It's to be New York," Ahmad continued. "You must make your effort to create the incident during the Venture's gala homecoming. There should be quite a few high ranking politicians attending the ceremonies. The homecoming will receive much national news coverage and if you are successful, you will turn it into a world event. It will elevate Islam to a new height in the eyes of the world.

"Ramon, belief in our faith is growing. More than two hundred million new believers have joined us in the last twenty years. There are still great numbers of Christians, but that is changing. The future is Islam, Ramon. We won't see it in our time, but one day the majority of the world will be Muslim. Who knows, maybe one day the whole world will be called Islam!" His eyes glowed with fervor.

"It will come about because of the sacrifice of Muslims like you, Ramon, people totally dedicated to Allah. Our way encompasses personal faith and piety, the creed and worship of the community of believers, a way of life, a code of ethics, a culture, a system of laws, an understanding of the function of the state — in short, guidelines and rules for a life in all its aspects and dimensions. It cannot fail, thanks to Muslims who are dedicated to the *Sharia*, the Way."

Ahmad had begun pacing, unable to remain seated. His voice dropped.

"I want to tell you something personal now Ramon— something that I feel you have the right to know. Many years ago, Ramon, I fell in love with a beautiful woman. We were both members of the same unit. Both of us were very dedicated to Allah and to what we could do to elevate Islam in our way.

"A time came when it was decided that she would be the best choice for a special mission. We knew in the future we would need people placed in different countries and, although it broke our hearts, she was sent to Spain and later was able to immigrate to the United States.

"I didn't know at the time, that she was pregnant. Shortly after arriving in the U.S., to continue her cover, she met and married an American military man. He knew she was pregnant and agreed to raise the child. Unfortunately for him, his health was bad and he died not long after the child was born.

"She had a son, Ramon. Need I continue any further?"

"You're telling me that you're my father?" Ramon said with amazement.

"I would have told you before," Ahmad said, "but I first wanted to know you, as a man. I wanted to see your reaction to our mission and feel your dedication to Allah. Please forgive me for my selfishness. I didn't get to be with you as you became a man but I praise Allah for allowing me to spend these few short days with you. I'm very proud to see that you truly are as dedicated as your mother."

Ramon felt tears sting his eyelids.

"I salute you, my son," Ahmad said as he embraced Ramon. "For what you are about to do, Allah will surely seat you by his side."

With that, he turned and walked away. Ramon attempted to follow, but one of Ahmad's men intercepted him. "He didn't have the courage to say goodbye, Ramon. He asked me to return you to the landing and to tell you how sorry he was that you didn't have the chance to know each other better."

Matt and Lee had spent another wonderful day together. Rio was such an exciting place and they vowed to return one day to spend more time there. The important thing was that they were together. They would have the rest of their lives together.

To get the lay of the land, they first drove up to *Vista Do Corcovado* the view from Corcovado, the location of the famous statue of Christ with his arms outspread. From a distance, he appeared as a large cross on the mountain. From the lookout deck at the base of the statue, the two viewed the most spectacular scene in Rio.

Off in the distance were the mountains that jutted up out of the sea. Directly to the front stood Sugar Loaf Mountain which stood as a lone sentinel protecting the bay and the city from the open onslaught of the sea. The city completely surrounded the bay, separated from the water by a narrow continuous ring of beaches. The lovers had chosen a marvelous spot to see everything.

They stayed for hours, then continued their exploration of Rio.

The afternoon sun dictated their appearance at the most famous beach in the world, Copacabana. Lee had to tantalize Matt with the latest in swim wear.

"I really love that suit you *almost* have on," was Matt's first response.

Copacabana Beach was so crowded with people that they had a hard time just finding a place to pitch their umbrella. Brightly colored umbrellas dotted the sand as far as they could see in both directions. In the background, skirting the beach, stood a solid wall of twenty-story buildings.

They eventually had to get out of the sun, not being accustomed to it. Gathering the picnic basket that Lee had acquired, they decided to return to the bungalow for some private quality time.

The drive took about ten minutes to the bungalow where they parked out front. The love making started in the car with several heavy-duty kisses, but when clothes began to be discarded, they laughed and agreed that they better continue in the bedroom. Approaching the door, Matt said, "I forgot the wine in the picnic basket. I'll grab it."

Returning to the car, he reached for the basket. Lee opened the bungalow door.

A horrific explosion ripped away the entire front of the small dwelling.

Matt spun toward Lee, a scream forming deep in his chest. He felt himself lifted by the blast that hurled him a dozen feet from the car. He struggled to get up but discovered he couldn't move at all.

As the blackness of unconsciousness closed over him, he thought of Lee.

Blazing light blinded him as he tried to open his eyes. Everything around him blurred dizzyingly. Several angels hovered over him. He closed his eyes hard several times, attempting to clear his vision. Slowly the angels began to take on a more solid appearance.

"He's coming around," said a male voice. "I want a head and chest workup right away and check response again of his pupils."

"Yes, sir," another angel replied, hurrying away.

Once again the blackness settled over Matt as he lapsed back into unconsciousness.

"Hey there!" he heard. "Time to wake up."

Matt slowly opened his eyes. Sharp pain pierced his head from the light. A policeman sat at the foot of his bed.

A doctor leaned over him while a nurse pumped up the cuff strapped around his arm.

"Do you know what day it is?"

"Yeah," Matt replied fuzzily. "It's Thursday."

"Well, you've only lost a day, which is understandable

considering what you've gone through," said the doctor. "This gentleman would like a few words with you."

The doctor and nurse left the room.

"Do you feel like answering a few questions?" the officer asked. "I can return later if you wish."

Matt felt confused. Why was this guy here?

"What happened?" he asked.

"You were injured in an explosion."

With that, it all suddenly flooded back. He had just reached for the picnic basket when. . . "Lee!" he cried out as he violently sat up. Nausea jolted his stomach, but that wasn't the worst of it. Matt felt as if something had just reached into his chest and torn his heart out.

His eyes clouded over as the grief overtook him. He stared straight ahead, looking directly through the inspector. Tears began to run down his face.

The inspector stood and said, "Forgive me, I can see this isn't a good time. I'm very sorry about your lady friend." He left the room, quietly closing the door.

Lady friend. *Friend?* He pictured her face. He could hear her laugh as they talked together. Smell her soft skin against him. Feel her lips as they pressed against his.

"Oh! God!" he cried. He broke into heart-wrenching sobs.

33

On the afternoon of September 24, the Venture left Rio. Only that morning, the captain had been notified by the Rio police that one of his sailors, Matt Blackthorn, had been involved in an explosion. Halliday learned that Matt was okay but there was one fatality. This would require Matt's being detained for a short period for further questioning.

A representative of the American Embassy would also investigate. The police assured the captain that Matt would be released in about a week and he would be put on a plane for the U.S. Halliday sent one of his staff ashore to confirm the report.

Chief Zabrinski was walking about now and, although his shoulder wouldn't heal for some time, he insisted on being allowed to leave the sickbay. The gunny, however, refused to take the bodyguard off Zabrinski. The chief reluctantly agreed and the Marine corporal became his second shadow.

The chief returned to his desk in the master-at-arms office and was looking through the drawers attemping to uncover something that might help him remember.

His conglomeration of strange dreams had continued to grow. Johnson, his assistant master-at-arms was sitting at a nearby desk.

"Hey Jack," Zabrinski said. "Let me tell you about a recurring dream I've had each night since I was shot. Maybe you can make some sense of it. I sure as hell can't."

"Sure, Chief, I hope I can," Jack responded.

"Okay, Jack, put on your imagination — here goes. I'm sitting in a coffee house when the door opens and in walks a guy leading a camel with a real strange hat on. The guy isn't wearing the hat, mind you, the camel is. The guy walks up to me, and I can't remember what he is wearing but he has a dogging wrench stuck in his belt. He says to me, 'I just ate Rue.'"

"That's it?" Johnson replied. "Boy, Chief, that is about the craziest dream I've ever heard of. You know though, just before you were shot, you had me send a dogging wrench to the Navy crime labs to be checked for prints and blood samples."

"Well, let's see the lab report, Jack, maybe we're getting somewhere at last," the chief said.

Johnson searched the files for ten minutes. "I can't find anything on that wrench, Chief," he finally admitted.

"You personally sent the wrench and paperwork off?" the chief asked.

"Well, Chief," Johnson replied, "I was going off duty as I recall. I had my relief take care of it. I do recall filling out the request though."

"Who was your relief?" The chief was getting steamed.

"I don't recall . . . just a minute," Johnson said, "let me look at July's duty roster."

Opening the duty roster for the month in question, he ran his finger down the list. Below his name appeared AE3 Roper.

"It was AE3 Roper."

"Get him up here," the chief ordered.

Roper was at the chief's desk five minutes later.

"Did you send the dogging wrench off along with the request paperwork before we left Cannes?" the chief asked.

"What dogging wrench and request?" Roper responded.

"Don't you remember that night when you came in to relieve me on watch, and I told you to take care of the dogging wrench right away?" Johnson said.

"Oh that, sure," Roper answered. "I don't recall any paper work but I put the wrench back in the bracket." He pointed at it.

The chief exploded. Before the fire storm cleared, Johnson had redone the paper work and personally delivered the package to flight operations, to be on the next plane out.

The chief's comment to Roper was something about his location when the brains were handed out.

34

The final scheduled demonstration at sea for foreign visitors was to take place on September 27th off the coast of Recife, Brazil — a two hour at-sea fire power demonstration by all three ships. A considerable amount of ordnance would be expended. The G-Division crew would be "bustin' their butts," as they liked to say, the night before the show.

This was the opportunity Ramon had been waiting for.

It was easy for him to grab one of the small Mark 12 baker bomb skids to move his cruise box. They were all over the hangar deck that night. He casually pushed the skid to the coffee mess.

He waited for two of the crew to finish their coffee break. As soon as the coast was clear, he dragged his cruise box out and strapped it on the skid. It appeared just like an ordinary box of 2.75 inch folding fin aircraft rockets.

He pushed it across the hangar deck and onto the nearest bomb elevator. It was about to descend to the second deck with more empty skids that were needed for bomb assembly there. He remained aboard the car and, arriving on the second deck, pushed his skid off and up the passageway toward the nuclear weapons area.

There was so much activity with the ordnance assembly going on, that he could have led a donkey through and no one would have paid any attention. Pushing the skid onto the elevator next to the nuclear weapons spaces, he locked the wheels and pulled the box off. He was in the process of dragging it over to the edge of the elevator car when he heard the voice.

"Hey, what's up Ramon?"

It was Vito, one of his friends from the crew.

"Oh, I get sick and tired of never being able to get into my cruise box in the coffee mess, Vito, 'cause someone is always sitting on it, so I'm going to keep it down in the well."

This wasn't an uncommon place for storage of ordnance gear so Vito didn't think anything unusual about it.

"Here," he said, "I'll give you a hand, then we gotta haul ass to the fire bomb storage. We just got word they want six assembled and filled for tomorrow's demo."

"Thanks," Ramon said as they muscled the box down the ladder and left it sitting against a bulkhead.

It took the crew about three hours to assemble the fire bombs. They were placed on the Mark 21 charlie bomb trucks and lined up on the hangar deck where the Napalm and gasoline would be added. Ramon wasn't usually involved in that step so he did his disappearing act. His stomach was calling to him and he went to the chow hall to eat.

The meal for the evening was chipped beef on toast which the crew fondly called shit on a shingle or SOS for short. Ramon actually liked it. It was a lot better than some of the other stuff they came up with.

Forty-five minutes later, Ramon was opening his cruise box and pulling out the gear bag. To avoid any unnecessary attention by having the lights on in the well, he used a battle lantern he took from a bulkhead on the mess deck.

Opening the gear bag, he pulled out the welding kit and opened the box. He discovered that instead of a cutting torch head, he had been given a welding head.

"Shit!" he swore softly. The plan was ruined.

How would he get hold of a cutting torch now?

He remembered all the welding gear in the machine shop down on the third deck.

He quickly put everything back in the box and climbed out of the well. Going to the nearest ladder, he made his way to the machine shop. He walked right in as if he worked there. There was a guy in the back working on a lathe but most everyone else had probably left for the day. As he scanned the shop, he found what he was looking for.

The welding gear was mounted on a bulkhead behind a heavy metal screen door. It was still unlocked. He looked across the room to make sure he hadn't been noticed. The guy was occupied measuring something. Quickly opening the door, Ramon grabbed a cutting torch head and held it down by his side. The guy hadn't looked up yet. Ramon was out of the machine shop within seconds.

There was one more thing he would need before he could begin. It was called a Red Devil, a type of blower used to vent bad air when paint, or chemicals — or welding — was in progress.

Going forward to the paint locker, he simply checked one out without any questions. There were never any questions when it came to safety in the Navy. He assembled all the gear in the well, then went to his compartment.

Around zero three hundred, he quietly got out of his rack and, with his clothes in hand, went to the head and dressed. He made his way to the elevator well.

Setting up the Red Devil on the mess deck, he ran the suction end of the hose down into the well and the exhaust to a nearby air duct labeled OUTBOARD. It was common to see these Red Devils around the ship so he wasn't worried that it would cause suspicion.

He returned to the well, assembled his equipment and began to cut a hole through the elevator bulkhead next to the nuclear weapons spaces.

Chief Zabrinski slept fitfully as the images of his repetitive dream began to take form.

For the hundredth time, he found himself sitting in the coffee house. The door opened and in came the guy. This time however, the *man* was wearing the strange hat. He still had the dogging wrench stuck in his belt. The guy walked up to Zabrinski and said, "I just ate rue."

The dream didn't end there like it normally did. The guy continued to the bar and sat down. He took off the strange hat and laid it on the bar stool next to him.

The chief saw himself pick up his cup of coffee. Looking into the cup, about to take a sip, he saw the image of the camel floating on the surface. The dream ended there.

35

The door to the hospital room opened and Tom Barnes poked his head inside.

"Could you use a little company, Matt?"

"Hey, Tom," Matt greeted the big man, as he entered the room. His voice sounded flat.

Frank entered shortly behind Tom with a tentative smile on his face. They pulled chairs next to the bed and sat down.

"So, what's the prognosis?" Tom asked.

"They're just keeping me here under observation until tomorrow, then I'll be free to leave." Matt replied quietly. "How did you guys find out so quickly?"

"The captain of the Venture," Tom said. "He wasn't aware that Lee was also part of the group. "The whole team is sorry about Lee, Matt. I know that the two of you had become very close. We're all going to miss her."

Tom's voice sounded tight. He blinked twice and cleared his throat.

"The terrorists are obviously worried about your interfering with their plans," Tom continued. "You must have gotten close to their man and didn't know it. Anyway, we need to get you back aboard that ship as soon as possible.

"The Venture is scheduled for arrival in New York Harbor on October third. That gives us just six days. We feel that the terrorist will attempt something there. It's the perfect situation. Lots of people, including important politicians, in a city with a population of millions, and . . . "

"Yeah, and remember their words," Frank interrupted.

"When the eyes of the world are watching."

"I don't know what you expect from me," Matt snapped. "I'm at a brick wall. I've tried everything I can think of to discover who this man could be. I've climbed and walked through every compartment and space on that damn ship looking for something suspicious. I've watched and talked to everyone who could shed any light on the matter and still nothing.

"I'm almost half afraid to talk to you guys any more. Two times I've almost been killed by the bastards and now, Lee," he paused, obviously swallowing hard. "She was the best thing that ever happened to me and now she's gone." He clamped his eyes shut.

"Hell," he added, "I haven't even seen one of the bastards yet but they sure as hell know who I am."

"I can explain that," Tom said. "I was contacted by the French police a while back. When they investigated the attack on Frank at Lee's apartment, they discovered several bugs. The terrorists probably heard everything we ever said and know every member of our group. Their earlier attempts on you and Lee and now this, shows that they had to get you out of the picture before you could interrupt their operation."

"They were probably responsible for Mike's death as well," said Frank. "Considering the personal vendetta attack on me, we believe that we were recognized and followed shortly after arriving in Cannes."

"It all boils down to this. They know we're aware of the sleeper. They know the captain of the ship is aware. They know who we are but we don't know who they are." Tom sounded grim.

"Our only course of action is to put you back into the picture. If their man aboard the ship feels threatened, he may, if we're lucky, make an attempt to take you out again, exposing himself."

"Gee thanks," Matt said.

"We are convinced," Tom continued, "their plan will be catastrophic in proportion. To be that big, it will have to have something to do with the nuclear aspect. The weapons or reactors are the only choice.

"Iraq's obvious efforts to obtain weapons grade materials and their lack of cooperation with the NATO monitoring teams over the last few months simply indicates their intention to create a nuclear incident of some sort.

"The Nuclear Task Force, with its nuclear reactors and nuclear weapons is in the international spotlight for the moment. It all fits together perfectly."

Matt suddenly blurted out, "The nuclear this, the nuclear that, blowing up this, destroying that. Here we are. We're supposed to be the good guys and yet we're cruising around the world with the explicit purpose of showing as many countries as possible how ultimate our power could be. Have we gone insane? Is the whole world crazy? Just think of how many people would still be alive if it weren't for the nuclear crap."

Tom and Frank watched in disbelief. Matt's eyes grew larger, becoming glassy as he continued. "There is Hiroshima,

Nagasaki, Chernobyl, Three Mile Island, on and on and on. Oh, how I hate what the word nuclear has done to mankind! Now it has taken Lee from me!"

He suddenly stopped, realizing he had lost control. Tom and Frank closed their mouths.

"I'm sorry," Matt said, regaining his composure, "I guess I'm really shaken over Lee's death."

"Yeah, I'm sure that's all it is," Tom said as he patted Matt's arm. He glanced at Frank with a slightly raised eyebrow.

Tom, using his NSC influence, took care of the details between Matt and the Brazilian police. By that afternoon, Matt found himself on one of the Venture's airplanes, en route to the ship.

Frank and Tom watched Matt's plane leave the Rio airport. "I think he's teetering right on the edge," Frank said.

"I think he might have already gone over," Tom said. "I just hope he can hold together long enough."

36

Ramon was limited in the amount of time he could work at cutting through the bulkhead. There was too much activity around the mess deck as the crew prepared for still another fire power display. The Venture was scheduled to pass San Juan, Puerto Rico in another day and an unscheduled display had been ordered by the captain.

The night following the Puerto Rico demonstration, Ramon completed cutting through the first bulkhead. Removing the section he cut out, he picked up the battle lantern and leaned through the hole. The lantern illuminated a vast void that dropped thirty or forty feet. Grabbing the opening, he barely prevented himself from falling into the blackness.

"Damn!" he swore. He waited for his heart rate to return to normal.

The next bulkhead stood about six feet in front of him but

this was going to necessitate building some kind of makeshift bridge to span the space. The ship was two days away from its gala home coming and he wasn't ready yet.

He was running out of time and he knew it.

The next night he had to be through the second bulkhead.

Looking at the situation, he decided that if he could find a steel ladder, he might be able to weld it down creating a bridge across to the second bulkhead. The problem was, every ladder that he knew of was already welded down and he had neither the time nor could afford the risk of moving the welding gear.

He would have to explore until he found something that would do the job. He put away the gear after tacking the plate back over the hole. At least if someone looked down in the well, the hole wouldn't appear obvious.

Spending several more hours looking, he finally gave up in exhaustion and returned to his rack hoping to get two hours rest before reveille.

Matt spent the day after his return to the Venture visiting with the chief. Zabrinski could see a marked change in Matt. He felt such compassion for him and his loss. He made every effort to console Matt and eventually changed the subject of the conversation from Lee to his dream.

He filled Matt in with the new parts of the dream and tried to make some sense of it but Matt was preoccupied and spent the conversation staring around the compartment. He contributed nothing at all and after mumbling something about nuclear this or that, wandered out of the master-at-arm's office.

The next morning the Venture said goodbye to the Dogeet as it broke from the Task Force for its home port of Charleston, South Carolina.

The day was a busy one for everyone. There would be one more air demonstration. It was to be just off the coast of New York City, late that afternoon. The Venture and the Tracker would then enter the harbor early the next morning for the gala homecoming.

The show wasn't to be a public display but a special demonstration for the President of the United States. He would be accompanied by the Assistant Secretary of Defense for Administration and Assistant Under Secretary of State for Political and Military Affairs. Of course the entourage would include the President's personal staff and a number of the media.

The visitors arrived early that afternoon. The uniform of the day was dress whites. A Captain's inspection was held on the flight deck as the President and Rear Admiral Drew were invited to inspect the crew.

Next came the airshow, as the guests viewed from the observation deck on the 011 level of the island structure. It was probably one of the better shows presented on the voyage, leaving the visitors impressed by the flying skills they witnessed. The crew's having practiced it thirty-one other times did help a little.

The officer's mess glittered that evening with silver and crystal. Champagne flowed liberally.

"Fantastic display this afternoon," the President told Captain Halliday.

"Thank you, Sir. I'm honored to have you aboard."

The crewman pouring champagne knew there wouldn't be any SOS on the table tonight.

"Mr. President," Halliday continued, "with your permission, Sir, I have an idea for another demonstration of our ship's readiness."

"Certainly."

"After dinner, then. I'll give the order. We'll go up into the island to watch."

At twenty-two thirty that evening when everyone had retired, and most were already snoring, the 1 MC system came alive with the dreaded clanging of the emergency bell.

"GQ! GQ! GQ! All hands man your battle stations!"

"This is a drill — Repeat! — this is a drill!"

"GQ! GQ! GQ! All hands man your battle stations! Set condition Zebra!"

It was followed by the strange phrase "Blue Nose Team!"

Then the whole announcement was repeated once again.

The ship suddenly came alive. The crew threw on their clothes as fast as they could. Those with emergency stations very far away, ran toward their battle stations with their clothes in their hands. In four minutes, condition Zebra would be set.

Condition Zebra required the closing and dogging of every waterproof steel door and hatch on the ship. Once closed, access was prohibited until the completion of the drill. Each man had to be at his assigned station in those four minutes. If not, the penalty was an automatic Captains Mast.

37

Chief Zabrinski sat at his desk in the master-at-arms office. It was about 22:15 but he wasn't ready to retire. He had sat there for hours going over the dream. It *had* to make some kind of sense and by *damn* he would figure it out.

Taking off his hat, he laid it upside down on the table and wiped his forehead. Hot this evening, he thought. Leaning on his elbows with his chin in his hands he contemplated the important parts of his dream.

There were the words — man, hat, camel, wrench, rue.

"Screw it!" he said surrendering, and stood up. As he reached for his hat, he noticed a small piece of paper protruding from behind the hat band.

"What's this?" he murmured.

Removing it, he unfolded the paper. The words leapt out at him.

Hat - Caf - Rue - Wed - 8pm - Eat - Ioh

His head began to spin like a spring coming unwound. He saw the captain - Young's body - the wrench - Ramon - the cup - the camel - the letter - the Cafe Rue - the man named Hat - the gunny - the cottage - the window - Ramon and two other men - the projector screen - the screen with blueprints of a reactor - the man reaching for the weapon - the flash of the muzzle.

He remembered. He remembered it all now. Ramon Isaban was their man. What could he have done to the reactor or what was he doing at this very moment? Jumping up, he started out the door.

"Come on, Corporal!" he ordered, "we've got to hurry."

No sooner had the words left his lips, than General Quarters sounded.

Ramon reported to second deck aft, the meeting point of the nuclear weapons loading team, referred to by protocol as "Blue Nose."

There were nine members on the team. One nuclear weapons officer, two nuclear weapons technicians, four aviation ordnancemen, and two armed Marine guards.

When Blue Nose was in progress, absolutely no one was allowed to enter the area of the weapon. The Marine guards, at the direction of the officer in charge, had the authority to shoot anyone who interfered in any way. It had never happened but the potential was there.

When Ramon arrived, the nuclear weapons elevator was just arriving, bringing a Mark 67 up onto the second deck. It sat on the Mark 33 charlie bomb truck, the heaviest non-powered bomb truck the Navy used. It had to be heavy to handle some of the larger weapons that weighed over two tons.

It was equipped with dual hydraulic cylinders that allowed the cradle the weapon was strapped to, to be pumped up to the bomb rack of the transporting aircraft. It was also equipped with four heavy duty solid tires.

The one thing that it didn't have was self power. This was the chore of the loading team. Each member of the team was assigned a specific location on the truck. The entire movement of the weapon was done to a very strict protocol. The ordnance-men were the pushers during the movement of the weapon. A movable tongue provided guidance and was operated by one of the nuclear weapons technicians. Guiding the 33 charlie was about the same thing as guiding a child's wagon, on a larger scale.

The officer and the other technician walked on each side. They carried their loading manuals and technical loading data for the particular aircraft used.

One of the Marines walked to the front and one to the rear. Next to the nuclear weapons elevator was the ordnance elevator. The team moved the weapon onto the elevator and tied it down with special tie-down straps. The elevator was activated and ascended to the hangar deck.

The team then moved the weapon to the port side number four aircraft elevator. Nothing else was allowed on the elevator except the weapon and the team. Once again, they tied down the bomb truck. The officer in charge gave the command and they ascended to the flight deck.

The chief entered the hangar deck ordnance office and immediately demanded to know where Ramon Isaban's general quarters station was.

"He's on the Blue Nose team, Chief," one of them responded.

"I just saw them go up the number four aircraft elevator with a nuke. They're probably going to demo a load for the great white father."

"Oh my God!" The chief felt the blood drain from his face. He grabbed the phone and dialed.

"Bridge," came the reply.

"This is the Chief Master-At-Arms speaking, let me talk to the captain," the chief demanded.

"He's with the President on the flight deck," came the response.

"Well, get him. This is an emergency," Zabrinski snapped.

"We're buttoned up here, remember Chief, condition Zebra."

"Can't you call him?"

"Not where he's at, Chief, I can see them walking toward the Island. I'll send a man down right away but it will take a few minutes to get through the Zebra doors. What number are you at, Chief?"

The chief had already hung the phone up and was on his way out the door.

"Stick close, Corporal, I might be needing you."

They ran to the number four elevator and, locating the operator, told him to bring the elevator down to take them up.

"Can't do that, Chief," the operator replied. "The only man authorized to use this elevator is the officer in charge of the nuclear weapons team. Not even the Admiral could call it down."

Turning in panic, the chief, followed by the corporal, began to run across the hangar deck toward the number three elevator.

The moon was blocked by an overcast sky, making it almost pitch black on the flight deck. The loading team were being guided by the red lenses of their flashlights. Each member carried one.

The idea began to take shape in Ramon's mind while they

pushed the weapon forward. By the time they arrived at the aircraft he had it all figured out.

The technicians began the loading sequence.

"Bomb truck tied down at all points," one said.

"Tied down port," came a response.

"Tied down starboard," came another.

Every single movement was enacted after being read off the check list by one of the technicians. The weapon was ready to be lifted to the bomb rack. Ramon's job, at this time, was to climb into the cockpit and confirm the position of the various power and armament switches.

The technician stood in sight of Ramon and loudly called up each step.

"Check master battery switch — off."

"Master battery switch off," Ramon replied.

"Check weapons selection switch — off."

"Weapons selection switch on guns, switching to off," Ramon replied. He turned the switch to the "Bombs" position.

"Nuclear weapons arming box, 'Off' — 'Locked' and 'Sealed'."

"Nuclear weapons arming box, 'Off' — 'Locked' and 'Sealed'," he repeated. He broke the wire seal and moved the switch to the "Armed" position.

"You're clear to load the weapon," the technician announced to the loading team.

Ramon's duty at this point was to exit the cockpit and assist in the final loading. While he waited for the technician to call out the steps, Ramon had quickly pulled all circuit breakers in the cockpit except the ones to the weapons system. As he climbed out of the aircraft, he switched the master battery switch to the "ON" position.

When the umbilical cable was attached to the weapon, he knew it would electrically align the accelerometer with the barometric fuse. He would only have to remove one access cover and unplug the accelerometer. The final step would be when he turned the barometric pressure switch to zero.

If he had been taught correctly, that would be the last breath he would ever take, and the final moment for the Venture and New York City.

Slowly, the team jacked the weapon up underneath the aircraft. A firm snap confirmed that the bomb lugs locked into the bomb rack.

"Attach umbilical plug," came the command.

"Attaching umbilical plug," Ramon responded.

Holding his red light on the cannon plug, he put his ear against the weapon. Pushing the cannon plug into the socket, he heard the sound of the accelerometer as it rotated into alignment.

"Umbilical plug attached," he called out.

At that point, the technician turned to the officer in charge and saluted.

"The weapon is loaded, sir!" he said crisply.

The captain hadn't taken into account how dark it would be when they loaded the weapon. There wasn't much point in hanging around the observation deck, so he called it a night for the prestigious visitors. After all, he didn't want the credit if the President of the United States caught a cold standing in the night breeze.

He returned to the cab where he could overlook the flight deck until the exercise was complete.

"Very well!" the officer in charge said, "You may unload the weapon."

The technician began to read off the steps for the removal of the Mark 67. A very heavy cloud now drifted between the ship and the moon. It was so dark that Ramon had trouble seeing either of the Marines.

They always stationed themselves at least ten feet away from the weapon. He was sure they couldn't see each other. He noticed the one nearest the edge of the flight deck was looking down at the bioluminescence of the water.

As the technician continued to read, Ramon began to move very slowly toward the Marine. When the weapon had been released from the aircraft and was back on the bombtruck, he made his move.

Ramon savagely struck the Marine in the throat with his fist, catching him completely by surprise. The man grabbed for his throat in pain and in the process dropped his rifle. Ramon stepped closer and pushed the Marine off the flight deck. The Marine, unable to scream, fell helplessly the ninety feet to the water.

Picking up the automatic rifle, Ramon walked directly back to the loading team. Switching the safety off the rifle, he also selected the fully automatic mode. When he came in view of the second Marine, he raised the rifle and fired a burst, killing him outright.

Everyone on the loading team immediately panicked. Running in every direction, they were quickly swallowed up by the darkness. The sound of the automatic rifle fire was carried away by the wind blowing across the flight deck. The captain and officers in the cab were unaware that anything had occurred.

The sound was heard, however, by the men on station in the catwalk along the edge of the flight deck. They saw the flash of the muzzle but couldn't see a thing after that.

"Cab, this is the catapult operator."

"Go ahead, catapult."

"Something strange is going on with the nuclear weapon

team. I'd bet my next month's pay that I just heard automatic weapon fire."

"Shit!" the captain replied. Turning to his orderly he said, "Get out there on the 0-11 and put a spot light on the weapon."

"Aye aye, sir." The Marine hurried away.

"Call the Marine department and advise them we have an emergency here. Bring them up the number three aircraft elevator and tell them to have their weapons loaded," he shouted.

Zabrinski and the corporal arrived on the flight deck and began making their way toward the island. Where was the weapon being loaded?

Suddenly out of the blackness, a dark figure ran directly into the corporal. Both sprawled on the deck. The sailor immediately jumped up and, as he ran for the catwalk, he yelled, "You guys better get the hell down! Some crazy son of a bitch just shot a Marine over there!"

A spotlight flashed down from the island, the beam slowly moving across the deck until it came to rest on the nuclear weapon.

Ramon crouched behind the weapon. He had removed the panel and discovered that he didn't have the correct tool to unplug the accelerometer. He turned the barometric pressure switch to zero but it wouldn't function as long as the accelerometer was attached.

He couldn't think. Sweat beaded on his forehead and began to trickle into his eyes. Think. *Think.*

The spotlight illuminated him. He panicked and picked up the automatic rifle. He shot out the light and most of the windows in the cab forcing everyone to dive for cover.

It wouldn't be long until the Marines charged the flight deck. It would all be over then.

He squatted next to the weapon, trembling. Steam drifted up from the catapult channel. The attachment device that hooked to the aircraft when it was launched stood only two or three yards away.

It was a crazy idea but it might work.

A pilot was subjected to over three Gs while being cata-pulted off the flight deck. If he could somehow throw the weapon off with it, that would surely activate the accelerome-ter. The more he thought about it, the more convinced he became that it would work.

Grabbing the tongue of the 33 charlie he let the brakes off and began to pull. His back felt like it would break but the bomb truck just wouldn't move. He tried repeatedly but it was no use.

He slumped back down next to the cart, exhausted. The wind died momentarily. He could hear men running across the deck. He remembered the tie-downs. Shining his red light at the truck, he realized it was still tied down in the back. Quickly releasing the tie-downs, he began once again to pull at the truck.

"Help me, Allah," he cried.

As Ramon strained with all his might, the truck began to move, ever so slowly. With the super-human strength of commitment, he finally positioned the truck at the attach-ment device of the catapult. The catapult operator spotted him. The operator stared as Ramon boldly strapped the tongue of the truck to the device used to pull the aircraft. Comprehension dawned on the man's face as he began to realize what Ramon was attempting. He opened his mouth to shout.

Chief Zabrinski and the corporal had approached as close as they dared and the corporal was attempting to get into a good enough position to get a shot off with his pistol.

The number three elevator arrived on the flight deck and the Marines began their approach, working their way from one aircraft to the next in the dark. They moved slowly, unsure if there might be more than one man. The gunny led the Marines. Soon they came upon the chief and the corporal.

"What the hell is going on, Chief?" the gunny yelled, buffeted by the wind.

"It's the guy I've been after, Gunny," the chief yelled back. "He's one of the men that shot me. At the moment, I wouldn't be surprised if he isn't trying to detonate that nuclear weapon he's captured. You've got to get him before he succeeds!"

"Don't worry Chief, we'll get him."

Gunny figured if they hit the weapon with rifle fire, it might set off the filler charge but not the nuclear device. He didn't know if this guy could set off the nuclear device or not, but at this point he couldn't wait to find out.

"Advance and fire!" he shouted to his men as he stood up and began firing toward Ramon.

Ramon completed wrapping all four tie down straps around the launching device and the front of the truck. It might not hold but he had no other choice.

Suddenly the air around him filled with the sound of bullets as rounds ricochetted off the deck and the weapon. It was like a fireworks display, only he knew better. Dozens of sparks lit up the flight deck all around the immediate area.

Picking up the automatic rifle, he jumped from the Mark 67 into the catwalk that lay just below the flight deck level. He almost landed on the catapult operator. Another sailor stood beside the operator.

"Activate that catapult!" Ramon demanded, pointing his weapon at them.

He could see the whites of their eyes in the darkness. Nevertheless, both shook their heads slowly from side to side. Ramon shot one of them point blank. Turning to the other, he put the rifle muzzle under the man's chin and screamed into his face, "I said activate that catapult!"

The operator swallowed hard. Sweat saturated his shirt

in the cool night breeze. He turned and brought the pressure up on the catapult.

Up in the island a red light came on indicating activation of the catapult. Everyone peeked over the cab's shattered glass, trying to see what Ramon was doing.

Through a brief break in the cloud cover the moon suddenly illuminated the flight deck.

The catapult activation light turned green. The sudden whooshing sound filled the air as the catapult fired.

The captain and crew in the cab watched in horror as the yellow bomb truck, with the nuclear weapon strapped in its cradle, violently hurtled down the flight deck.

The Marines stopped shooting and all stood staring, frozen in that moment as the truck gained tremendous speed and became airborne off the front of the carrier.

Next came the white hot, blinding explosion as the weapon detonated. Men on the flight deck and in the catwalks were tossed backward like leaves in a strong wind.

Soon the black enveloped the night once again.

38

The National Security Council's capabilities for acquiring information were second to none. They had the very latest in computer equipment and were tapped into any and every department of government that could provide them with something useful.

While a case was active computer technicians keyed the equipment to intercept and transfer any incoming information related to that case.

This was how Tom's group stayed abreast of the situation on the Venture. Several days prior, he had received a copy of a request for a lab workup on some kind of wrench. It had been sent to the Navy crime lab by the chief master-at-arms aboard the Venture. Since the Venture's name was present, a copy was routed to Tom's office.

He contacted the lab and requested a copy of the results of the lab workup. It was on the way.

It was in connection with the death of Mike Young and requested a cross match of tissue and blood on the wrench with that of the deceased. It also requested identification of finger prints found on the wrench.

Tom felt angry at being kept in the dark. The captain of the Venture was supposed to be cooperating with NSC. Now it appeared otherwise, that the ship was doing its own investigation. He wondered how much Matt had not told them.

Frank burst into his office.

"We've intercepted a news release on its way to the wire services. Some kind of incident occurred aboard the Venture last night."

He handed the copy to Tom.

United news release — Oct 2 — On board the aircraft carrier Venture - somewhere off New York -

An incident occurred during the President's visit aboard the nuclear carrier Venture. A liquid oxygen cart used to refill aircraft oxygen systems exploded while being serviced, at about 11:00 tonight. It apparently had a leak which came in contact with a small amount of oil on the flight deck.

One Marine and one sailor were killed at the scene, and one Marine and one sailor are missing and presumed to have been blown off the flight deck by the explosion.

United's reporter, who was aboard at the time, said all involved were part of a special nuclear weapons loading team and that a weapon was being loaded at the time.

The Navy emphatically denies any connection between the explosion and any nuclear weapon whatsoever.

"Frank, get us a flight to New York immediately," Tom ordered. "And make sure Halliday knows we plan to come aboard. First though, I want to see the results of the lab tests on the wrench. I think we're about to nab Mike's killer."

Twenty minutes later, Tom held the lab report in his hands. It indicated a match between the tissue and blood samples found on the wrench and those of Mike Young. Exactly what Zabrinski had suspected. They'd found the murder weapon.

The finger prints were another matter. The computer matched a thumb print with one taken during an investigation associated with a nuclear facility in 1975. It was found in the apartment of one James McMurphy, convicted saboteur. What possible connection to the Venture?

"We need to know more about this, Frank. See what you can dig up. I want to know which nuclear facility and where," Tom said.

Frank headed for the Com Center and returned to Tom's office an hour later.

"Here is about all I could find on short notice," he said.

Tom took the copies and began to read.

Reactor Safety -

In October, 1988, reports revealed that the Savannah River plant (South Carolina), a nuclear facility making tritium for warheads, had experienced at least thirty serious reactor accidents between 1957 and 1985, including the melting of a fuel assembly. These accidents were kept secret, and it was only after a study of the plant had been released that news of the plant's failures filtered out. The study found incorrect installation of parts, ruptured seals, and other equipment failures, and inadequate maintenance procedures.

It was later determined that some, if not all, of the accidents were the results of tampering by persons employed by the plant who belonged to the organization called the "A-A-A". The Army Against the Atom is a fanatically dedicated organization of anti-nuclear supporters whose goal is to create incidents that will incite negative opinion and fear. It is the A-A-A's belief that only through injuries or death of innocent people can enough news coverage be generated to support their cause.

One James McMurphy, a late 1960s hippie and war protester, was found guilty of the Savannah River plant tampering. He received a prison sentence of forty years and is currently incarcerated at Attica, New York State's maximum-security correctional facility.

"Where is Attica prison?" Tom asked Frank.

"It's near Buffalo."

"Get us on a flight to Buffalo and notify the prison we want to talk to James McMurphy," Tom directed.

By early afternoon, Tom and Frank touched down at the airport in Buffalo. A car from their Buffalo office waited for them and took them directly to the prison.

Approval for the questioning of James McMurphy had been obtained enroute. They were ushered into a visitor's room and soon McMurphy shuffled in.

James McMurphy was a small man, so thin that his prison uniform hung on him like a sack. He was totally bald on top with long gray hair on the sides. His years in prison had been hard on him and he looked about twenty years older than the fifty indicated on his fact sheet. He wore round wire rimmed glasses popular in the sixties.

"What can I do for you gentlemen?" he asked as he sat down.

Tom and Frank produced their credentials.

"I am agent Tom Barnes and this is agent Frank Pierce. We are both with the Crisis Intervention Group of the National Security Council. We would like to ask for your cooperation in an investigation currently underway," Tom began. "I understand that you've exhibited a marked change in your attitude toward society, and the possibility of parole now exists for you.

"By cooperating, you might contribute to saving thousands of lives and, of course, this would show favorably toward your parole board. You've already served sixteen years of hard time with good behavior and it's possible that your sentence could be reduced. I can't promise anything but we'll try. What do you say?"

McMurphy sat there a moment before speaking. "Will anything I say be made public?"

"No," Tom replied.

"What do you want to know?" he agreed.

"Tell me about your cell of the Army Against the Atom at the time of your arrest," Tom said.

McMurphy laughed.

"What cell? You talk like the A-A-A, was a large nation-wide organization. Well, *Army* does make it sound big, huh? Hell, I was the only one who worked at the plant. I was always a sucker, demonstrating for nearly anything. At first it was causes for nature, then feeding the poor, then when the Vietnam War broke out it was anti-war demonstrations. Hell, I even went with Jane Fonda to Vietnam to protest.

"On that trip, I met this guy who introduced me to the A-A-A. There weren't any cells, just me. He told me there were several other individuals involved but for obvious reasons, it was best that identities were not known by the various members."

"What did this guy look like?" Frank asked.

"Ah, hell, he was real young and skinny, couldn't have been more than twenty-three or twenty-four. He had blond hair. He reminded me of one of those surfers. Course a lot of guys dressed like surfers in those years.

"He would show up at my apartment unannounced and bring me orders from the group that planned all the activity.

"He was real smart though, and very dedicated to the A-A-A. He hated anything to do with atomic research. Hell, he even hated the word *nuclear*.

"He acted as a contact person. He always complained that he wasn't allowed to *do* anything like me. You know, sabotage a machine, break something, spill something. He used to say that someday no matter how long it took, he would show everybody.

"They were probably right to hold him back. He seemed a bit *too* gung-ho. You know, one of those overdoers. Anyway, he was the only guy I ever met."

"What was his name?" Tom asked.

"He called himself Tim Moore but you can bet that was a phony. He sure was smart though," McMurphy repeated.

"You've said that twice now," Tom said. "What made you think he was so smart?"

"I met another guy at the plant who convinced me that if he were to meet the person who devised all the accidents, that he would shake his hand. He gave me the impression that he wanted to help us out. I invited him over to my apartment to meet Tim.

"Tim didn't hang around long. He was really pissed at me and said the guy could be an undercover agent. I didn't see Tim anymore, 'cause shortly after that I was arrested. Tim was right, the guy was an undercover cop for some government security thing. Anyway, you know the rest."

Tom thanked McMurphy for his cooperation and promised he would submit a favorable report for his parole hearing. On their way back to the airport, Tom called the NSC Communications center on the car phone. He requested the name of the arresting agent during the Savannah River investigation of 1975.

As the NSC car pulled up to the terminal at Buffalo, the car phone rang.

"Tom Barnes," he answered.

"Com Center here, sir. Concerning the Savannah River investigation of 1975, the arresting agent's name was Mike Young."

"Thank you," Tom said, hanging up. He dabbed his forehead with a handkerchief. Worry lines pulled his eyebrows together.

"It was Mike Young," he said to Frank.

"Oh shit," Frank said. " This is beginning to make sense. Matt's little display in the hospital in Rio sounds just like McMurphy's description of Tim. Matt is the right age now to have been Tim. He must have recognized Mike and thought

Mike would remember him, so he killed him. And we put Matt right in the middle of our operation."

"Looks like we've got two nuts on that ship to worry about," Tom said.

39

The Gala homecoming.

The morning after Ramon's valiant attempt found the routine on the carrier returned to normal. The results of the night's activity had vanished through the efforts of the flight deck crew. Not a single sign remained of the previous night's accidental explosion.

The arrival of the Venture and the Tracker was promoted as a spectacular event. Not since the tall ships flotilla during America's bicentennial, had a publicized event gathered so many people.

Six New York Harbor fire-fighting boats led the procession. Each boat had all water nozzles spraying large streams into the air. An unprecedented collection of the world's last great sailing vessels followed. They all fell in behind the two

237

returning ships forming a spectacular display of present and past.

Leading the armada of sailing ships was the U.S. Coast Guard training ship Eagle. After gliding past an honor guard of warships, the Venture and Tracker anchored in their respective locations, officially bringing to an end the circumnavigation of the globe by the nuclear task force.

About twenty thousand smaller boats studded the harbor, and the crowds in New York City were estimated at more than four million. Indeed, a gala homecoming.

Ceremonies would continue on the flight deck of the Venture throughout the day. In the late afternoon a ceremony was scheduled, for the mayor of New York to present the key to the city to the captains and crews of the two returning ships.

Captain Halliday, in a pause between festivities, relaxed in his in-port cabin thinking about the previous night. He felt angry and embarrassed about the incident and hoped that his excuse about a liquid oxygen cart would be accepted without any further coverage by the media accompanying the President.

Immediately after the explosion, he had sent some of the master-at-arms force to block off passageways leading to the visitor's quarters. He could have completely kept the lid on the incident had it not been for one news man snooping around on the flight deck after the incident. Fortunately, the man arrived after the explosion and hadn't witnessed the incident.

The reporter had hidden in a head near the bridge in hopes of getting a scoop on the behind-the-scenes action during a general quarters drill. He had overheard some of the crew discussing the involvement of the nuclear weapons loading team and was busy making notes when discovered. He was immediately escorted to his quarters.

The captain understood and appreciated how lucky he was. How lucky they all were.

Chief Zabrinski filled him in on Ramon Isaban. Ramon's service jacket lay open on the desk.

If the terrorists had better information concerning the status of the nuclear weapons, thousands of people, or more, would be molecules now. The guy was dedicated; Halliday had to give him that.

He was definitely glad the asshole had been blown over the side by the blast. It avoided all the legal crap that would have followed the incident. That alone would have given the Navy a massive black eye.

How would they have ever explained how some guy who looked like an Arab and whose mother immigrated from Spain, had gone completely through bootcamp, "A" school, aircraft munitions school, and nuclear weapons loading schools, *and* all the accompanying security checks without one person seriously questioning his background.

No, he thought, I can't complain about the outcome. His eyes narrowed. I hope the sucker realized, as he was falling that ninety feet, that the blast that knocked him off the flight deck was conventional and not nuclear. Too bad for his cause that the weapons all looked the same. If his sources had been better he would have known that protocol prohibited loading an active material weapon with the President on board.

The phone shocked him out of his contemplation.

"Sir, this is the O.D. There are two men from the National Security Council. Mr. Tom Barnes and a Frank Pierce. Their credentials appear in order. They are asking to speak to you."

"Very well," the Captain replied. "Have them escorted to my cabin."

"Aye aye, Sir," came the reply.

The captain called the master-at-arms' office and directed Chief Zabrinski to report right away. Zabrinski walked in right after Barnes and Pierce, and Halliday introduced them.

The Captain asked Chief Zabrinski to go over how he had

uncovered Ramon Isaban, followed him and subsequently been shot while overhearing the reactor training session at the cottage. The chief explained that due to his head wound, no one else had known about Ramon until he recovered his memory the previous night.

"You understand, gentlemen," interjected Halliday, "that this conversation is for this group only. The Navy will emphatically deny everything. All right? Continue, Chief."

"Last night, during a general quarters drill, a nuclear weapon was being loaded on the flight deck. Somehow Ramon Isaban, one of the nuclear weapons team and, I might add, the terrorist we have all been searching for, took control of the situation.

"He was able to get an automatic rifle away from one of the Marine guards and in the process, probably killed him and threw his body off the flight deck. Before the situation was over, he had shot two other men. Through some quite ingenious moves, he armed and launched the weapon off the flight deck with the catapult. The G forces created by the catapult, were sufficient to detonate the weapon," the chief said.

"He exhibited astounding creativity under such pressure," added the captain. "I wish he had been on our side."

"That's probably the reason he made it this far," said Tom.

"Fortunately for us," said the chief, "he wasn't aware of Navy protocol regarding the presence of high ranking U.S. dignitaries during a loading exercise. It states that while the visitors are aboard, only practice weapons may be loaded for demonstration. Practice weapons are externally identical to the real thing, including the explosive charge used to detonate the radioactive material. The nuclear device, however, has been removed.

"Basically, he launched the equivalent of a one thousand pound bomb about two hundred feet out in front of the ship, which detonated without damage.

"The blast blew Isaban off the catwalk. Even if he had survived the blast, it was still a ninety foot fall to the water," said the chief.

"So in conclusion, gentlemen," the captain added, "Our threat for the present is over and we can enjoy the festivities of the Gala."

"I wish that were true!" Tom said.

40

"Chief, have you got the response to your request for lab work on the dogging wrench?" Tom asked.

"How did you know about that?"

"Our computers picked it up. I asked for a copy from the lab and it indicated a match of the blood and tissue samples."

"Then I was right, Ramon killed Mike Young," the chief said proudly.

"I wish that were true, Chief," Tom continued. "One thumb print on the wrench was tied in with an organization called the A-A-A., the Army Against the Atom. They were a fanatical anti-nuclear organization back in the sixties. The print was thought to belong to a Tim Moore.

"We went to Attica prison where we interrogated a convicted saboteur. He gave us a good description of the man. He informed us that he met the man on the anti-war trip with Jane Fonda. A further check revealed that the arresting officer was a young undercover agent on his first assignment, named Mike Young. On our way here, I had our computer compare the thumb print with those on record of the Venture's crew."

"And?" the captain said.

"The print belongs to Matt Blackthorn," Tom concluded.

"No!" said the chief, "I can't believe it."

"I'm afraid there's too much supporting evidence." Tom continued, "One, his records indicate that he was involved in the anti-war demonstrations in the sixties for a short time.

"Two, he was on the Jane Fonda anti-war trip to Vietnam.

"Three, he's the right age and description of Tim Moore, the young man introduced to Mike Young by the convicted saboteur.

"Four, the computer has identified his thumb print.

"I'm afraid there's no question about it," Tom assured them. "During our last meeting with Matt at the hospital in Rio, he most definitely exhibited an unstable condition. During our conversation, he made several negative comments about nuclear related things. At the time, we felt it was due to the loss of his friend, Lee Curtis. That obviously wasn't the case."

"It has probably been his intention, from the day he came aboard the Venture, to create some kind of nuclear incident," said Frank.

"Captain, we feel it's imperative that you take him into custody immediately. There's no telling what he might be doing, even as we speak!" Tom added.

"Chief!" the captain ordered.

"Yes, sir!" the chief replied as he got up to leave the room.

"Captain, we've known and worked with Matt for the last couple of months and, with your permission, we would like to accompany the chief. Perhaps when confronted with three people he knows he may be more willing to cooperate. It could prevent any violence," Tom added.

"By all means, Mr. Barnes," the captain replied.

Leaving the captain's cabin, they began a search of the ship. They first tried Matt's living compartment. His cubical was empty, which was to be expected at that time of day. Next, they went to the master-at-arms office and from there the chief called around to see if any of his men had seen him while on watch. They all knew him personally. No one had seen him.

The chief suggested they walk through the mess deck area since the chow hall was still open. They split up and walked back and forth between the tables checking the faces.

Matt *had* to be aboard somewhere. Zabrinski was worried. What would Matt do? Last night's explosion might have pushed him mentally over the edge. They checked every sponson and open port where someone might seek isolation. Eventually they worked their way to the flight deck. Still no Matt.

"I have an idea," Zabrinski told the others. "Matt was temporarily assigned to the M.A. force but after last night, he may have reported back to his regular department."

"Where's that?" Frank asked.

"The Reactor Laboratory Department," the chief said.

"You mean he could be down there messing around with one of those reactors, in his frame of mind?" Frank asked, surprised.

He didn't get an answer. Both Tom and the chief realized the impact of what he said and were scrambling for the ladder that led below decks.

As they hurried off the flight deck, the crowd was beginning to assemble for the "key to the city" ceremony.

Down they went into the belly of the Venture. One ladder brought them to another and then another. Eventually they arrived at the reactor spaces.

"Did First Class Petty Officer Blackthorn come through here?" Zabrinski shouted breathlessly. His shoulder throbbed and he felt lightheaded.

"No, sir," the Marine sentry answered. The chief was baffled.

Then it hit him like a dogging wrench.

"Mike Young was killed outright," he said to the other two. "It would have been easy for Matt to arrange a little accident and perhaps no questions would have been asked. We know Mike must have seen something. But maybe Matt didn't kill Mike because of what he remembered from the past but for what he might have *recently* seen. Come on, follow me."

He led them to the void next to the number six reactor, the place where Mike's body had been found.

As they entered the void, they could hear someone moving about. A low voice mumbled indistinctly.

A maze of pipes entered and exited the bulkheads. Little arrows on them indicated the direction of flow for whatever they carried. As the three men got closer to the person, the talk became louder.

"I'll show them the proper respect for nature!" the voice muttered. "You know you just can't fool around with this stuff. It's just not natural, more, it's an out-and-out insult to God! Someone has to help God explain to them! Look how America scared the world to its knees with this shit! It's time America got a little dose of its own medicine.

"Everything was so wonderful." Matt's voice cracked. "Lee and I could have been happy the rest of our lives. I could have gotten out of the Navy and Lee and I could have been married. We would have been happy, I just know we would have, but no, somebody had to split the atom. Somebody had to make a weapon from it to scare somebody else."

It was obviously the voice of someone gone mad. The rambling continued.

"What do we do now?" the chief whispered.

"We need to find out if he's armed first," Frank responded.

As they approached, Matt spun around like a mad dog.

He was almost unrecognizable. His hair stuck out in every direction. Grease covered his hands and face. He had obviously been busy. His eyes were glazed over and spittle ran down the side of his chin. He had the look of a crazed, trapped animal.

"Hi, Matt," Tom said as they approached. "We've been looking for you."

"Stand back," he screamed.

"It's okay, Matt," Tom said as he stopped. "Look, Frank's with me and so is Chief Zabrinski."

"Hi, Matt," Frank added.

"Hello, Matt," the chief joined in.

"We've been looking for you, Matt," the chief added. "We wanted to have a good ol' fashioned game of poker and knew you'd want to play."

"Yeah, it wouldn't be any fun without you, Matt," Frank added.

"Can't," Matt said, "I have to finish. Just one more thing to do. Then they will see, you all will see! You'll all be so proud of me!

"Look, see!" he said pointing to the pipes. "It took me almost a year but I've nearly finished."

"Finished what, Matt?" Tom gently asked.

"Why can't you see?" he snapped. Then he threw his head back in laughter. "Oh, I'm sorry, of course you can't see, it all looks quite normal doesn't it?

"Well you see that pipe there, it comes out of the number six reactor core housing. Normally there's not a pipe there at all, but I was pretty clever and installed it so well that even the reactor guys didn't notice.

"And look," he said, "how it runs down through the deck.

Just cutting that hole so perfect took me a week of nights. Then all I had to do was put putty around the fitting and paint it, and it looks welded doesn't it."

"Yeah it was a terrific job," Tom said, acting excited. "You know, Matt, we're real stupid about these technical things. Just for our benefit, could you explain what all of this means?"

"Okay," Matt responded, childlike. "That pipe goes to that valve." He pointed. "It's an emergency valve to shut off the recirculation of the contaminated heavy cooling water. But you see, I got this neat idea and disconnected the return pipe and put my pipe on there. It goes to the collection tank for the steam catapult.

"A while ago, I opened the valve and by now, all of that contaminated heavy water should have drained into the holding tank. Pretty good idea huh? The reactor will automatically shut down any minute now. Maybe they can stop a melt down but they can't stop me!"

"Can't stop you from what?" Tom asked.

"Why, from dumping it in the bay, Tom." he said as he pointed at the box on the bulkhead about a foot from his hand.

Looking, they saw a switch box. Above it the label: CATA-PULT HOLDING TANK DOOR SWITCH

One button was for opening, the other for closing.

"Just think," Matt continued, "Three hundred gallons of extremely high radioactive heavy water dumped right in the middle of New York harbor. I bet everybody will be scared after that to use nuclear power. Right, Chief? Right, Frank?"

"But lots of people will be hurt Matt, think of all the little children and animals," Tom tried.

"Yeah I know, but what about all the little children and animals that lived in Hiroshima, and Nagasaki, and Chernobyl. If the scared people here won't allow the technology in America then nobody anywhere else can get it. It all really comes from here you know. Everybody just steals it from America. It's for the best, don't you see?"

Frank moved behind Tom with the hope of being able to jump forward and overpower Matt. Matt saw him move and began to reach for the button.

"Please don't push the button, Matt!" Tom said reaching for his pistol.

"Don't worry, Tom," Matt replied. "It won't hurt any place else, just here."

As his thumb touched the button, the deafening sound of Tom's pistol reverberated through the void, echoing from one chamber to another, as if to replay the scene over and over.

The sound slowly faded out at the other end of the void.

"So tell me, Captain," the reporter asked, as he pushed the microphone toward Captain Halliday. "With eight nuclear reactors and all these weapons and destructive forces around you, don't you sometimes worry that the wrong guy might get aboard to create havoc?"

"Impossible!" the captain said, exhibiting an expression of total assurance. "Not with the Navy's multiple security checks and our constant state of alert. If you had any knowledge of the Navy, sir, you wouldn't be asking such a ridiculous question."

Ramon released the rope he had used to lower himself to the water. He had hidden in Fire Bomb Stowage long enough. Quietly, not to attract attention, he swam away from the Venture.

"Impossible!" the captain repeated. He looked the reporter squarely in the eye as he said it.

Intrigue Press

Bringing you the finest in Mystery, Suspense, and Adventure fiction.

If your favorite bookstore doesn't carry Intrigue Press titles, ask them to order for you.

Most stores can place special orders through their wholesalers or directly with us. So, don't go without your favorite books — order today!

And if you liked this book, recommend it to your friends!